Time for Audrey Buchanan
sex, love & timing

a novella by jillian conley

3 mythreesisters
publishing

ISBN-13: 978-0615970318
ISBN-10: 0615970311

Published by My Three Sisters Publishing

www.my3sisters.com

Break-ups are fucking brutal. It had been over two weeks since I left Chase's condo for the last time and I was still a hot mess. My agent was on my fucking case because I hadn't finished editing the final book in my series and the only time I left my apartment was to restock on wine and donuts. I had zero desire to go out and I hadn't returned my friends' calls in several days. Hopefully, tomorrow I'd finally get a swift kick in the ass to accomplish more than finishing a bottle of wine on my own.

I awoke the next day to a pounding on my door. When I first woke up, I was sure it was my head pounding from all the wine I had drank the night before, but then I heard Nikki's loud Italian voice screaming through the door, demanding I let her in. I dragged my half-naked ass to the door and opened it. Nikki took one look at me and said, "You look like fucking hell."

I started to cry. Nikki walked into my apartment and up to me then smacked me across the face. I yelled out, "What the fuck was that for?"

Nikki said with attitude, "Snap the fuck out of it. You are acting pathetic over a piece-of-shit man. Get the fuck over it and take a fucking shower because you smell like hot garbage."

As I held my cheek, which was still tingling from Nikki slapping me, I said like a child while stomping my feet, "But I don't want to!"

Nikki asked with attitude, "Do you want me to smack you again? I will. Go fucking shower and then we are going out to get some food in your stomach. It looks like you haven't eaten in weeks."

I quietly said, "I've eaten."

She asked, "What have you eaten? Fucking donuts and wine?"

I quietly responded, "No."

"Don't lie to me. I'm staring at two empty boxes of donuts and like a dozen empty bottles of wine on your kitchen counter."

I said, "I had to eat like a thousand donuts because Chase never let me eat them!"

Nikki said, "Yeah, because he was a fucking controlling asshole! Go shower and fucking shave your legs and bikini line. You look like a God damn gorilla."

I rolled my eyes and said, "Fine, you asshole," as I walked to the bathroom. As I showered, I realized Nikki was the swift kick in the ass (more like swift smack across the cheek) I had been telling myself I needed. Nikki was right and I couldn't wallow in my misery. I had to get on with my life. I had written out all my feelings already and when I was finished, I'd told myself it was time to let go. Now, I needed to follow my own advice and actually let go.

I washed my hair and armpits, but I didn't shave. It would be just too much work and I was kind of enjoying playing with the long hairs on my ankles. The hairs had gotten so long that they had become soft. It was more like fuzz than it was hair. I wanted to see how much longer I could go before I had to shave my legs again.

After I got out of the shower, I walked out of the bathroom. Nikki was cleaning up my disaster of an apartment. I told her she didn't need to clean, but she said she was utterly disgusted and couldn't stand it. I didn't say anything further because inside I didn't mind that she was cleaning up. The less I had to do, the better.

Once I was dressed, we headed out the door. As we walked to the local tavern that we frequented often, I realized that the shower I had taken and the sun shining outside had already made me start to feel better. When we walked inside the tavern and sat down, I ordered a vodka with 7Up, but Nikki told the waitress I couldn't drink. I asked, "Why the fuck not?"

Nikki said, "You need to stop drinking so much."

The waitress looked at me funny, but I said, "I'm good, give me a vodka 7Up."

Nikki said, "No, she's a recovering alcoholic. Don't bring her any booze."

The waitress looked confused, so I said, "I am not a recovering alcoholic. I am recovering from a break-up, so bring me a very stiff vodka 7Up."

The waitress asked, "Are you sure?"

I said, "Yes."

After the waitress walked away, Nikki said, "You shouldn't drink for a while."

I responded, "I'm fine. I'll just have two drinks, maybe three."

"Audrey, I'm being fucking serious. You need to fucking snap out of this shit."

"Nikki, I'm fine. I've gone through the depression period and I am good now."

"You are not good. You are a hot mess."

"I'm fine. I promise I'll clean up my act."

"He's not worth you wasting your time. Look what he did. He walked away from you like it was nothing."

I said with aggravation, "He did it for his career."

"Listen to yourself. Why would you stick up for him?"

"Nikki, he broke my heart, yes, but it doesn't mean he is a bad person."

"He's a womanizer. He used you when it was convenient for him and then walked away."

"Let's not talk about Chase anymore."

"Fine, but he's the reason you look like you've been hit by a truck."

"I do not look that bad."

"You do. You look fucking anorexic, you have bags under your eyes, you are as hairy as a gorilla, and if I didn't make you shower, you'd still smell like hot garbage. And your apartment - your apartment is fucking disgusting."

"I just needed a swift kick in the ass and you were that. I promise I'll get my ass in gear now."

Nikki asked, "Have you been writing at all?"

I responded, "Yes."

Nikki fished further by asking, "Anything good?"

"No."

"What the fuck? You haven't left your apartment in two weeks. You should have a novel written by now."

With hesitation, I said, "Well, I wrote the story of Chase and me."

Confused, Nikki asked, "What?"

"I sat and wrote the entire story of my relationship with Chase."

"Why would you do that?"

"Therapy. To get it out. To go through it all, then let go."

"When did you finish it?"

"Like a week ago."

"Apparently, you haven't let go."

"It's harder than it looks. I'm trying. There's no surgery to fix anyone after a break-up. It takes time."

"You've had enough fucking time."

Nikki continued bitching at me until our food arrived. I ate a huge-ass hamburger and it was delicious. After we ate, Nikki seemed to calm down and stopped talking to me like an angry parent. She moved on to talking about the latest man in her life who she had met earlier in the week. She had found a new bald-headed tattooed hunk of hotness. As she was updating me on everything I had missed over the past couple of weeks, my stomach began to feel uneasy. I told Nikki my stomach was hurting so I was going to head home. Eating a huge greasy burger after not really eating much for two weeks was probably a bad idea. Nikki asked me to stay until she finished her drink and I agreed because it looked like she only had a few sips left.

Fifteen minutes later, Nikki hadn't finished

her drink and I could feel the gas moving through my intestines along with a little bit of sweat building on my upper lip. Nikki noticed the sweat and discomfort and asked if I was feeling okay. I told her I had to leave. Something was about to happen with my ass and I needed to get home before it did. She told me to go ahead and that she'd pay the bill and meet me back at my place.

I walked out of the bar and down the street in a scurry. Halfway home I had to squeeze my cheeks to hold in whatever it was that wanted to get out of my ass with vengeance. A block away from my apartment, a squeaker of a fart snuck out of my ass even though I was squeezing my cheeks tight. I started to walk even faster. I entered my building and ran up the stairs faster than I had ever run before. I was still squeezing my ass cheeks tight, but as I was fiddling with my keys to get my door open even the tight squeeze of my ass cheeks couldn't keep the angry shit from exploding out with force and I shit my pants.

I stood in my doorway full of embarrassment and I began to cry, but as I walked into my apartment, bow-legged with panties full of shit, I began to laugh. I couldn't believe I had shit my pants. It wasn't the first time I had done this, but it definitely had been at least a decade since I had walked with underwear full of poop.

I walked into the bathroom and turned on the shower. Still laughing, I took a long look at myself in the mirror and quickly my laughter turned to tears again. I looked like hell and I was standing in panties full of my own shit.

How could I let myself reach such a low? And over a man who had walked away from me like it was nothing. I needed to clean this shit up, literally, and pull my life back together.

I slowly pulled my panties off and dumped the mud pile that had gathered in them into the toilet. I then ran the water in my sink and put my panties in the warm water to soak while I got in the shower to clean the shit out of my ass crack. As I was lathering up my loofah with soap, Nikki walked into the bathroom. She said, "Fuck, it smells like shit in here." I popped my head out from behind the shower curtain and she continued with the question, "Did you shit your pants?"

I frowned as I said, "I did."

"Gross, are those your shitty panties in the sink?"

I nodded my head up and down as I said, "Yes."

"I'm sorry. It fucking stinks in here. I'll be out on the couch."

I finished cleaning the shit out of my ass crack and walked out to the couch. Nikki gave me a look like she felt sorry for me. I said, "I've hit rock bottom, haven't I?"

Nikki said with seriousness, "Audrey, you are a fucking disaster."

I said, "I know. I don't understand why I hurt so badly."

With sincerity, Nikki said, "Love, love hurts."

I asked, "How do I get over him? I don't want to be a disaster anymore."

Nikki said, "Go bang a random dude."

I smiled as I said, "You are nuts, Nikki. I'm

not going to go bang a random dude."

Nikki asked, "Why not? It works for me."

"Yeah, because your relationships last like two weeks and are purely sexual."

"Not true, I've been in love."

"You've fallen in love in two weeks? I think that's called infatuation."

"Hey now, you can fall in love in two weeks. You fell in love with Chase at first sight."

I said, "I did not."

Nikki rolled her eyes as she said, "You did too. You were all like, 'Oh, he sent butterflies through my body and shit.'"

I said, "That's called lust."

"No, you were in love with him. That's why you have been such a hot mess. Seriously, go fuck another guy and you'll be fine."

"Screw that and screw men. I think I'll be a lesbian."

"Audrey, you wouldn't know the first thing to do if you were to have sex with a woman."

I wasn't very confident as I said, "I'd figure it out."

Nikki said, "I'm setting you up on a date."

I asked, "With a girl?"

"No, you idiot. With a guy. He's my new boss. He's really nice and you could use a nice guy right now."

"Nikki, you just said I need to have sex to get over Chase - now you want to set me up with a nice guy?"

"You can have sex with a nice guy."

I said, "Nice guys are annoying in bed."

"Not always."

I said, "Yes, always. I've dated a few nice guys in my day and they were always asking questions and they are so insecure in bed. I need a man who is confident and knows what the fuck he's doing."

"I'm setting you up on a blind date."

I changed the topic. I wasn't ready to date in any way, shape, or form. I never rebounded from guys by jumping into dating someone new. I felt like I should take a little time to recover from the ridiculous whirlwind of a romance Chase played on me.

TIME FOR AUDREY BUCHANAN

A pparently, Nikki didn't listen to me when I said I wasn't ready to date yet and she set me up the following Tuesday to meet a guy named Wayne at Tavern on Rush. All I knew about Wayne was that his name was Wayne and that he was the Vice President of the company Nikki worked for. Nikki refused to give me his full name because she didn't want me stalking him on Facebook before the date and pulling out at the last minute. I hadn't been on Facebook in weeks. I was too afraid of seeing photos and updates of Chase's so I didn't log on at all to avoid the possibility of seeing him all happy and shit.

On Tuesday night, I got dressed up and put make-up on for the first time in weeks. I hailed down a cab and headed to Tavern on Rush. I wasn't sure how I was going to find this guy, Wayne, but Nikki told me not to worry because he'd find me. I wanted and needed to eat some good food so going out would be good for me, but to prevent any sort of spontaneous combustion from my ass I popped an Imodium before I left. I didn't think anything would come of me dating this Wayne guy, but I didn't want to end up with any embarrassment of shitting my pants again.

I arrived at Tavern on Rush and looked around. The name Wayne made me think of this old neighbor I had growing up who wore jorts and Hawaiian T-shirts. No guy in Tavern on Rush was wearing such an outfit so I was convinced Wayne was not in the building. As I stood, confused and looking around, a blonde guy with a rather large head came over by me and said, "Hi Audrey."

I could only assume this blonde man was Wayne, so I said with a little hesitation, "Hi, Wayne."

Wayne smiled as he said, "It's so great to meet you, Audrey. Nikki speaks highly of you."

I responded, "Nikki has told me nothing about you so I look forward to getting to know you."

Wayne walked over to the host's stand to let them know we were ready to be seated. I looked Wayne up and down, noticing that he had a nice body, but his head - his head was like the size of an extra large watermelon. I couldn't help but think of his poor mother and how she had had to push that big-ass head out of her vagina. I decided right then and there that I'd never carry this man's children for the mere fact that I was scared to death of pushing any baby out of my vagina, but a baby with a huge noggin was completely out of the question.

Although having this man's children was out of the question, eating a steak and drinking wine he'd bought for me was completely acceptable. Besides the larger-than-life head on Wayne's shoulders, he seemed to have a rather nice body from what I could see. He was blonde, though. I didn't like dating blondes. I had always been attracted to dark hair and features. Even though Wayne had a huge-ass head, blonde hair and light features, I tried to look past all of it and focus on his personality.

There was a bit of an awkward silence when we first sat down so I threw out some small talk and said how I was enjoying the fall weather. Wayne agreed, saying he was enjoying it too, but that he was more of a summer guy. That conversation was going nowhere so I asked Wayne if he was going to order wine. He had a bit more to say about this topic and decided we should order a bottle of wine. I was totally down. My tolerance for liquor had significantly increased in the past few weeks and I was sure I could take down a bottle of wine on my own. He ordered a bottle of Merlot, which was not my favorite, but it was a hundred-dollar bottle and he was paying for it, so I assumed I'd enjoy it.

After the waiter took our wine order and left, Wayne asked how long I had been single. This is probably one of the worst questions anyone could ask on a first date. I simply responded, "A few weeks."

Wayne dug for more information and asked, "Why did it end?"

I said with a little attitude, "My ex decided he needed to date multiple women to further his career so he left me."

Wayne looked a little taken aback by my answer and asked, "What kind of career did he have?"

"He was a dating and sex expert."

Wayne looked really taken aback by this answer and asked, "He was a what?"

"A dating and sex expert. He helps men become more successful with women in their dating and sex lives."

Wayne asked, "Really?"

I didn't want to be talking about my fucking ex-boyfriend Chase so I threw Wayne the same question and asked, "How long have you been single, Wayne?"

"A few weeks too. Caught my fiancée sleeping with my best friend when I got home from work early one night."

With my eyes widened I said, "Fuck, that fucking sucks."

"Yeah, it was brutal, but I can't wallow over it. I need to move on."

I asked, "So, am I the first date you've been on since you broke things off with your fiancée?"

"I went on a date last weekend, but that didn't go so well. I love committed relationships; however, I just want to date around and get my sea-legs back. I was with my ex for seven years."

"Shit, that's a long time. Welcome to the single life, Wayne, it's full of doubt, misery and a lot of bullshit."

Wayne chuckled as he said, "Sounds like it's going to be a great time."

I laughed as I said, "It gets old fast, but you will have a good time in the beginning. All new things are fun and exciting."

Wayne and I chatted a little longer about the single life. He did seem like the type that preferred to be attached, but had a positive outlook on being single. I wished I had his enthusiasm. I was still stuck on my ex Chase and had no desire to embrace the single life. After two glasses of wine, Wayne decided to tell me the story about the night he walked in on his fiancée with his best friend. The story made me want to stay sober because it made for some good ammo for my writing and I didn't want to forget the details. When he walked in on his fiancée and friend fucking, his fiancée actually suggested Wayne join her and his friend. Sounded like a storyline straight out of a porno to me.

When we walked out of the restaurant, Wayne asked for my number. I didn't want to give it to him, but I decided to after I reminded him I wasn't looking to get into a relationship anytime soon. He said he thought I was fun and he would like to hang out again soon. I could agree to that. He seemed like he just wanted to have some fun.

I got in the cab and headed home. My belly was full of wine and steak and I couldn't wait to get into my pajamas. I got home, threw on my pajamas and decided to log onto Facebook. I hadn't been on it in weeks to avoid seeing Chase and of course, the first person I saw on my home page was Chase in a photo smiling his balls off with two women. I clicked on his name and scrolled down his page seeing check-ins and photos with tons of women. I sat and tortured myself for a few minutes before deciding to delete his ass. Seeing him and his happiness would not help me move on.

After I deleted Chase as a friend on Facebook, I patted myself on the back and then took a look at my notifications. I had hundreds of notifications and nine new messages. I browsed the notifications, but they were just a bunch of nonsense. I then clicked on the messages and most were creepy-ass men saying, "Hey." I blocked them all, but then I saw a message from a guy named Ben who I had met about five years ago on a yacht out on Lake Michigan. I clicked on his message and it said, "Random, I know, but I thought I'd see how you are doing?"

I decided to respond and I wrote, "Random, indeed. I am doing well, Ben. How are you?"

I clicked on Ben's profile to see what was new in his world. Ben was hot and from what I remembered from that drunken day out on the yacht, he was a good kisser and pretty well-off. As I was stalking Ben's Facebook page, an instant message popped up from Ben saying, "I am doing well. I see you are no longer an aspiring writer, but you are a published author now."

I typed back, "You saw correctly. So what was with the random message?"

Ben responded, "I was bored one night and stumbled across your profile. Decided to take a look and say hello."

I asked, "Stumbled across?"

"Yes, stumbled across. What are you doing this weekend? Come visit me in New York."

Come to New York? I hadn't seen Ben in years and he just blurted out for me to come to New York. What the fuck was going on? I waited a few moments before I responded. I wasn't sure what to say because I kind of wanted to get the fuck out of Chicago for a weekend and I heard fall in New York is beautiful. I decided to respond, "Maybe."

Ben responded, "No, not maybe. I'm booking your flight right now."

I said, "Get the fuck out of here."

Ben asked, "Can I call you?"

I got up and poured myself a glass of wine, debating if I should allow Ben to call me. After filling my glass up, I responded to him with just my phone number. A minute later my phone was ringing with a New York number. I answered, "Hello."

As expected, Ben was on the other end of the line and he said, "Hello, Audrey."

I said, "What the fuck are you talking about me coming to New York?"

"I see you still have the mouth of a trucker. I find that endearing."

I said, "I'll take that as a compliment, but what's with the random invite to New York?"

"I know it is random, but I heard you are single, so come out here and I'll show you a great time."

I asked, "How do you know I am single?"

He responded, "I still talk to Nikki here and there on Facebook."

With my trucker mouth in full force, I said, "Fucking Nikki. So she put you up to this?"

"No, she didn't put me up to anything. She just mentioned it in a conversation. It was all my idea."

Not believing Ben, I said, "Sure it was. I'll think about New York and let you know."

"No thinking. I am online now looking at flights. Does Thursday to Sunday work for you?"

I responded, "Ben, this is totally ridiculous."

Ben said, "Come on, Audrey, live a little. If you get here and you are not enjoying yourself I will get you on the first flight back to Chicago."

I asked, "What are we going to do in New York?"

Ben asked with humor, "What are we going to do? It's New York City - there's a million things to do!"

"Ben, I just don't understand why you want to fly me out to New York to visit you?"

"I'm not sure where the idea came from, but it could be fun, Audrey. So just let me treat you to a romantic weekend away."

When Ben said the word 'romantic', I was totally turned off. I had no desire for romance, but maybe I needed some romance to remind myself that Chase wasn't the only man I could 'fall in love with'. I took a sip of my wine and after Ben asked why I was being so quiet, I decided to say, "I'm in for New York. Book me a flight."

Ben became very enthusiastic and while I was still on the phone, he booked me a flight. He emailed me the confirmation and then we discussed the many options of things to do while I was there. He said he'd plan it all out for us. I needed a weekend away from Chicago where I'd be spoiled and experiencing new things. Getting Chase off my mind was a must. My only worry was that Ben would have sexual expectations. I was nowhere near ready to sleep with someone. I wanted to be, but I just wasn't ready yet.

Thursday afternoon I was scrambling around my apartment trying to finish packing for my trip to New York City when my agent called me, screaming that she needed the final copy of the last book in my series. I told her I couldn't talk because I was frazzled trying not to be late for my flight to New York. Naturally, being the nosy woman that she is, she had all sorts of questions for me as to why I was going to New York City. I tried to explain as briefly as I could, but then said I had to go, assuring her that I'd send her the book before I left for the airport.

I finished packing and sat down in front of my computer, wishing I had been more organized so I didn't have to rush so much. While I was composing the email to my agent, the limousine company Ben had booked for me called and said they were out front. I felt even more frazzled so I just typed, "Here it is" and attached the file before pressing send, closing my computer and running out the door. I got downstairs and the driver took my bags before opening the door for me to get in the limo. When I got in, there was a chilled bottle of Dom Pérignon waiting for me, along with a Glazed and Infused donut topped with the letters NYC. This guy was good. He must've talked to Nikki or majorly stalked my Facebook page.

Whatever he'd done, I was happy.

I sipped on the fancy champagne and chowed down the donut after taking photos of them and putting them on Instagram and Facebook, of course. I was due for some bragging and hoped that somehow Chase would come across them. The first class seat on my flight was pretty awesome too, so by the time I landed in New York I had a healthy buzz and I wasn't nervous to see Ben.

Ben was waiting for me with a bouquet of white daisies - my favorite flower - when I walked into the baggage claim area. I hugged Ben hello and then walked outside to the limo. I gave Ben a smile while he poured me some champagne and then I asked what we'd be doing that night. He said he figured I'd be tired from traveling so we were just going to dinner. Plus, he had an early morning and long day planned for us. I was nervously excited for what was about to come.

The limo drove us the scenic route to Ben's ridiculously huge condo in Gramercy Park. I thought people in New York had small places, but not Ben. Wall Street must've been good to him. He showed me around and then brought my luggage into the guest bedroom. I was actually a little shocked that he wasn't expecting me to sleep in his bed with him and appreciated that he didn't make any assumptions. He told me to take as much time as I needed to freshen up before heading to dinner at a restaurant called Per Se. I asked if it was a nice restaurant and he said it was one of the best I would ever go to. After Ben left the room, I Googled the restaurant on my phone to make sure I chose an appropriate outfit to wear.

The restaurant looked fancy as fuck so I took out the nicest dress I had packed. I only had one really nice outfit so I hoped this would be the only fancy dinner we'd be going to over the weekend. After I was dressed, I stood and looked at myself in the mirror. I looked insanely skinny and pale. I felt a sense of disappointment in myself for allowing Chase to hurt me the way he did, and then I felt a lump growing in my throat. I didn't want to start crying so I took a deep breath and told myself to snap out of it. When I walked out of the bedroom and down the stairs, Ben was sitting on the couch, patiently waiting for me. He looked hot, all dressed up and it kind of made me mad that I wasn't feeling turned on. When Ben looked up at me, he smiled and said that I looked gorgeous. I needed to hear that more than he would ever realize.

The limo took us to dinner where we drank expensive wine and ate a nine-course meal. I was extremely stuffed and prayed my stomach would behave itself because I really didn't want to deal with shitting my pants again. The conversation with Ben was so nice. He seemed truly interested in me and what I was saying. He seemed like such a grown-up, which was the exact opposite of what I remembered of him on the yacht the summer I met him while he was visiting Chicago. I knew he was successful, but he seemed to really have his shit together.

We got home that night and Ben walked me to the guest bedroom before kissing me on the forehead goodnight. The kiss sent some flutters through my body, which was a good sign. The flutters made me long for more affection, but I just smiled at Ben and told him goodnight before closing the bedroom door. I put on my pajamas and washed my face before crawling into the insanely comfy bed. I reflected on how much of a gentleman Ben had been all night and knew that coming here was the right decision. I was still skeptical of his intentions, but grateful that he was being so kind.

I was really full and the bed was insanely comfortable, but I couldn't fall asleep. I kept thinking about the sensation I had felt when Ben kissed my forehead. The affection felt nice and it made me feel cared for, which was such a different sensation compared to the sensation Chase had brought to my body. I started wishing Ben was in this bed,holding me, nothing more; I just wanted to be held. I wanted the comfort of being in a man's arms. I decided to crawl out of bed and walk down the hallway to Ben's room. I lightly knocked on the door and Ben opened it. He looked sexy in his boxer briefs. If it weren't for Chase breaking my heart, I'd be all over Ben. I asked, "Can I sleep in here with you tonight?"

Ben smiled when he asked, "Did you have a bad dream?"

I giggled a little before I said, "I would just like to cuddle with you if that's okay."

"Of course, Audrey. Come on in."

Ben got into bed and held the covers open for me to crawl in next to him. I crawled in and the moment he wrapped his arms around me, I felt a sense of relief run through my body. My God, it felt so good to be held. I would be happy staying in his arms in bed all weekend if he'd allow it. I felt so much comfort in his arms that I fell asleep almost immediately.

I woke up in the morning still feeling the comfort of Ben's arms around me. I scooted my butt back to bring my body closer to his when I felt his hard dick poke into my back. It made me smile a little bit. Ben whispered in my ear, "Sorry, sometimes I can't control it."

I said, "Don't worry, it made me smile."

Ben was so nice and fucking sexy as hell so I wanted to crawl under the sheets and put his cock in my mouth, but I knew I wasn't ready. I just laid there cuddling with him as I felt his cock slowly lose its hardness behind me. We cuddled for a bit longer and then Ben told me we should get moving because we had a big day ahead of us. I asked what we were doing and he said to get ready to do some shopping. I thought to myself: *How am I not in love with this man and how has some girl not already scooped him up?* What was wrong with him? His cock didn't feel small when it was poking my back so I didn't think that was the problem. Now I was curious as to why Ben was still single.

I got out of bed and went into the bathroom in the guest bedroom to shower. Once I was ready, a limo picked us up and took us to a pastry shop called Milk Bar. We walked inside and Ben told me to pick whatever I wanted. Of course, I picked out a few donuts. We got back into the limo and he popped open a bottle of Dom Pérignon before mixing up some mimosas. I went to pull a donut out of the bag to eat it, but Ben told me to wait. I didn't want to wait; I wanted that delicious sugary treat in my mouth, but I trusted him.

I looked out the window, admiring all the buildings we passed by. New York had such a historic feel to it. I loved the old buildings and realized why it was considered one of the most romantic cities in the world. The limo pulled up in front of Tiffany's and I felt a smile grow on my face. I knew what was about to happen; we were going to have breakfast at Tiffany's just like Audrey Hepburn did in one of my all-time favorite movies, *Breakfast at Tiffany's*. Did Ben know that having breakfast at Tiffany's was always a dream of mine? He had to have talked to Nikki.

We got out of the limo and walked around eating our donuts, looking at the window displays. I felt so much happiness running through my body. I had to take a picture and check in on Facebook; this was way too historical a moment for me. Ben took a photo of me with my donut and then I posted it with the caption "This Audrey is eating breakfast at Tiffany's today!" After we finished our donuts, we went inside to walk around the store. A woman brought us to a secluded area and we sat down. I thanked Ben over and over for bringing me to Tiffany's and told him he had no idea how much it meant to me. While I was thanking Ben, the woman came back with a tray that had six different pieces of jewelry on it. Ben smiled at me and told me to pick my favorite. I said, "Oh, Ben, I can't. You've done so much for me already."

Ben said, "Audrey, pick one. I insist."

I smiled and pointed to the Tiffany Somerset Link Bracelet. The woman took it off the tray and handed it to Ben to put on my wrist. I smiled as I said, "Thank you."

Ben said, "Great choice. My favorite is this one so we'll take that one too."

The lady holding the tray asked, "The Elsa Peretti Snake Necklace?" to confirm that was the one he wanted.

Ben said, "Yes, this one with the black jade."

I cut in and said, "Ben, this is too much."

Ben said, "No, it's not. Let me put it on you." I allowed Ben to put it around my neck and I literally felt like I was living out a scene in the most romantic movie that ever existed. I smiled some more and gave Ben a small kiss on the cheek. I sat, enjoying wearing the fancy new jewelry when the woman asked to have the items back so she could wrap them up in boxes. I wanted to keep the necklace and bracelet on, but agreed because I wanted the little blue boxes that she'd be wrapping them in.

When we got back into the limo I asked, "Ben, why are you buying me these things and being so nice to me?"

Ben replied, "Audrey, my intentions are a little selfish..."

I interrupted Ben right away, voicing the first assumption that popped into my mind, "You just want to sleep with me. That's why, isn't it?"

Ben shook his head back and forth and said, "No, no, Audrey. I mean, I am a man and I'd love to sleep with you, but that's not why I wanted you here. And it's not why I am spoiling you."

I asked, "Then what is it?"

"For the past nine years I have completely focused on work. I've ignored personal relationships and only focused on making money. Now, here I am with millions of dollars and nobody to share it with. I'm ready to settle down, but it seems like all the women I've been dating are so fake. I saw you on Facebook one day and remembered how fun and down-to-earth you were when I met you. I decided I'd invite you out here to spoil you and get to know you better."

What the fuck was going on? I shouldn't question Ben because it made sense, but I had no idea guys like this actually existed. He must have a small penis. That had to be it. I simply said, "Well, Ben, you alone have restored my belief in men."

"Good. Now, let's get over this serious talk and get back to shopping."

Ben took me shopping at the best stores in New York City. I felt like Julia Roberts in *Pretty Woman* trying on expensive clothing and walking out with bags full of new dresses, shirts, jeans, jewelry, shoes, purses, and more. At one store, we had the stylist put together an outfit based completely around the Elsa Peretti necklace Ben had bought me at Tiffany's. I was full of excitement and gratitude and when I looked in the mirror I felt sexy for the first time since my break-up.

After a long day of shopping, Ben and I went back to his condo and snuggled up to take a nap. After our nap, I showered and got dressed up in my new outfit and Tiffany jewelry before heading to dinner at Jean-Georges. We were stuffed, but headed over to a rooftop bar to snuggle up under a blanket and take in a great view of the Empire State Building. It was chilly, but the comfort of the blanket and being near Ben kept me warm. Once our food finally settled, Ben said he had the best surprise for me up next. I couldn't even imagine how things could get any better, but I trusted his word.

We pulled up to a rather dark area and I thought to myself: *Crap, here it is. Ben seemed so nice, but now he's going to rape and murder me.* Trustingly, I followed Ben's lead, holding his hand and believing that rape and murder weren't on the agenda for the night. We went inside a building that seemed like an underground club. Ten steps inside, I realized why this was going to be the best part of the weekend. We were escorted in to a table up front in The Box, an underground type theatre of varieties. It was sexy, it was unique, and it was somewhere I had heard of and always wanted to go. The shows were amazing and so sexy. I actually felt my panties getting wet, which got me excited. The free sexual spirits, sexual innuendos, and lack of clothing made me feel like Stella getting her groove back.

When Ben and I got back to his place, I was feeling sexy and decided to kiss him. It felt good, but Ben backed off and said he knew I had had a lot to drink and he didn't want me to regret anything. I knew he was right, but I was feeling so good and I didn't want the feeling to stop. I thanked him for being responsible, but asked if I could still sleep next to him. He agreed that sleeping next to each other would be okay. The whole night he didn't try any funny business. This guy was such a fucking gentleman - or gay; that was still to be determined, I guess.

We spent all day Saturday outside in Central Park. The changing colors of the fall leaves were beautiful and the day was relaxing. Over our picnic lunch, Ben told me more about himself; his past and plans for his future. I really started feeling a connection with him and as we were rowing a boat around the pond, I leaned in and kissed him. When we pulled away from our kiss, he smiled at me and I felt little butterflies run through my body. The butterflies must've distracted me because when I pulled away and went to sit back down, I lost my balance and fell over the side of the boat into the water. It was freezing cold, but when my head came above water I couldn't help but laugh. Ben helped me back into the boat, laughing, then wrapped me in a blanket.

As I shivered and laughed, Ben rowed the boat as fast as he could back to the dock area. We got off the boat and walked back to the limo. When we got in the limo I took off my wet clothes and he wrapped me up in a dry blanket. We were still laughing. He pulled me into his arms to warm me up and then turned the heat on high in the limo. Ben joked that his kiss was so powerful that it had put me head over heels.

I scurried from the limo into Ben's building in only the blanket while Ben followed behind me with my wet clothes. When we got inside Ben's condo, he drew a bath for me in his gigantic bathtub. I patiently waited for the tub to fill up with water while I remained wrapped up in the blanket. He left the bathroom and once it was full, I got in. He knocked on the door gently before entering and bringing me a glass of wine. I asked if he wanted to join me, but he hesitated. I said, "I'm sober and asking you, so it's not the liquor talking."

Ben got undressed and it was the first time I was able to get a good look at his cock. It wasn't bad. It had a little girth to it, which probably came from the excitement of taking a bath with me. He settled in next to me and we sipped on our wine as bubbles multiplied in the tub from the jets. I moved closer to Ben and he pulled me in, wrapping his legs around me. I felt so much comfort in his arms and from being near him. How could a man so considerate exist? It made me want to be in love with him so badly. Although I was starting to feel ready to experience him sexually, I didn't feel a sense of overwhelming desire for him. As badly as I wanted to, it wasn't there.

So badly wanting to want him sexually, I went in for a kiss. Our kiss moved to a make-out session and soon we were grinding on one another. With my legs wrapped around him, he stood up and carried me out of the bathtub and out onto his bed. Still with bubbles all over our bodies we lay on his bed, making out a little longer. His cock was grinding up on the outside of my pussy, but not penetrating me. It didn't classify as dry humping because we were both wet with bubbles. I was turned on by the whole scenario so I whispered in Ben's ear, "Fuck me."

Ben looked at me with hesitation and asked, "Are you sure?"

I said, "Yes, I am so turned on right now."

Ben reached into his nightstand and pulled out a condom. He put it on and penetrated my pussy. Usually, the initial penetration felt amazing to me, but feeling his cock inside me freaked me out. I didn't want him to stop though. I wanted him to make me feel amazing sexually, like he had been making me feel so good all weekend. He moved his cock in and out of my pussy slowly and it felt good down there, but all of a sudden I felt an urge to cry. I tried so hard to hold back, but tears burst out of me. Ben pulled his cock out of my pussy and said, "I'm so sorry. I knew you weren't ready."

I said, "No, no, don't stop. I'm ready."

Ben said, "Audrey, you aren't and I knew that. I shouldn't have allowed this."

With tears running down my face, I said, "No, Ben, don't stop."

"Audrey, you just went through a very hurtful break-up. I knew that when I invited you. I didn't bring you here just for sex. I want to get to know you and I don't want to rush you into something you aren't ready for. It's okay."

I said, "No, no, it's not fucking okay. My ex is an asshole and you seem to be an amazing man. I want to have sex with you."

"Audrey, there's no rush. I'm glad you want to have sex with me, but it doesn't have to be tonight. I want to have sex with you when you are ready."

With tears running down my cheeks and boogers dripping out of my nose, I asked, "Why are you so fucking nice?"

Ben giggled a little before he said, "I haven't always been this nice. I've been a womanizer and slept around quite a bit, but I'm over that. I want to experience a woman fully and sex can wait."

As I cried even more I said, "I can't believe you've been so nice to me."

Sunday night, as I was waiting at the gate for my flight, I received a text message from my agent that said, "Be at my office at 9am sharp."

The first thought in my head was *crap, I am in trouble*. I knew I should have edited the final book in my series better before I sent it. I had had such a great weekend and it was just ruined knowing that I'd have to get up early and face a lecture from my agent. She was such a feisty bitch, but she did her job well so I had to show up without question. I arrived home and crawled right into bed. I set my alarm for 7:30 a.m. to allow myself enough time to shower before heading to my agent's office. In the morning, I took a shower and I was at my agent's office at 9am sharp.

My agent's assistant had me wait on the pleather couch until my agent was ready for me. I sat waiting, with my leg shaking nervously like a high schooler who'd been sent to the dean's office. I loathed getting in trouble and never took lectures well. I'd always tune out and then end up in more trouble for not listening. My agent opened her door and smiled at me. She said, "Come on in, Audrey," as she waved me into her office.

I wasn't sure what was happening. She was smiling. I thought I was in trouble, but her actions led me to believe otherwise. Maybe the final book in my series was better than I thought. I walked through the door and she welcomed me with a hug before shutting the door behind us. I sat down on a chair in front of her desk and she pulled out a bottle of champagne. I was really confused now. As she popped open the bottle of champagne she said, "Audrey, you have written your best story yet and I couldn't be more proud of you. I opened the document up and read the book in its entirety in one sitting. I cancelled meetings because I couldn't put it down and you know I never, ever cancel a meeting."

With confusion I asked, "Really?"

My agent responded, "It is the most moving and unique story I have ever read. I sent it to your publisher and Anna read it in one sitting, too. They want it on the shelves as soon as possible. I also sent it out to a friend who owns a production company out in Hollywood and she wants to buy the rights to the story to script it and make it into a movie."

As I sipped on the champagne, the confusion in my head stirred even more. I asked, "Would the first two books in the series be a part of the movie or just the final book?"

My agent responded, "What first two books? I'm talking about the story *Dating Chase Walker* that you sent me."

I asked, "What? *Dating Chase Walker*?"

"Yes, you sent me a manuscript called *Dating Chase Walker*."

I said, "No, I didn't."

"Yes, you did." My agent grabbed a stack of papers off her desk and handed it to me as she said, "Here is your story."

I flipped through a couple of pages before I said, "Fuck, I sent you the wrong document."

My agent asked, "What do you mean?"

"I was in a rush and I meant to send you the final book in my series, but I must've sent you this gibberish I wrote to get over my ex-boyfriend."

"Well, Audrey, this is the best mistake you have ever made."

I chugged the rest of the champagne in my glass and then said, "I can't publish this story."

My agent asked, "Why not?"

I said, "Chase wouldn't allow it."

"You don't think he'd love the exposure?"

"I guess, but he gets his panties in a wad over anything he's not in control of. This story represents our relationship through my eyes."

"Send it to him and ask him to read it, then let's move forward."

"I need some time to think on this. Can you give me a few weeks?"

"You have until Friday. Sleep on it, ask your friends, talk to Chase and then get back to me."

My agent and I sat and talked a little longer and then I left her office. I decided to go for a walk because it was a nice fall day and I had a lot to process. On my walk I realized I was by Nikki's office. I walked inside to see if she'd have some time to get an early lunch with me. The front desk gave her a call and they granted me access to the elevators. When I got to her floor I waited by the door for her to come and get me. She welcomed me with a hug and said she couldn't wait to hear all about my trip to

New York. I gave her a serious look and said, "Nikki, I really need to talk to you."

Nikki asked with concern, "Is everything okay?"

I said, "Yes, but I really need your advice."

"Okay, come to my desk with me and I'll see if I can take an early lunch."

I followed Nikki to her desk and then she left me standing alone by her cubicle. Gross, I was so glad I didn't have to spend eight hours a day in a tiny-ass cubicle. I'd go insane. I sat down in her chair and looked at the cubicle across from Nikki's. The entire wall space of the cubicle was full of baby pictures. Now, said like that, it sounds cute, like this woman really loved her babies; but no, these were not pictures of babies she knew. At least, I don't think she knew all these babies. They were pictures of babies cut out of magazines. It creeped me out a little bit. Why would someone fill their cubicle with pictures of babies cut out of magazines? More importantly, why hadn't Nikki told me about her crazy cubicle neighbor?

As I was sitting and wondering why this woman had so many pictures of random babies, Nikki's boss, the guy I went on the date with, Wayne, walked by. When he saw me he gave me a funny look as he asked, "Audrey, what are you doing here?"

I stood up and said, "Hi, Wayne, how are you?"

"I'm doing well. It's good to see you, but what are you doing here?"

I hesitated as I said, "Well, I'm dealing with a bit of a personal issue. I was walking by this office after a meeting and I am hoping Nikki can take an early lunch to help me out."

Wayne asked, "Is everything okay?"

I said with a bit of hesitation, "Yeah, I mean, I think so."

Wayne asked, "Where is Nikki?"

"I'm not sure where she went."

"Well, when she comes back tell her I said it's okay to take the rest of the day off."

I asked, "Really?"

Wayne said, "Yeah, get what you need figured out. It's just a bunch of number pushing here." Wayne let out a little laugh as he continued, saying, "It's nothing really important."

Nikki grabbed her things and we made our way toward the elevators. Once we got in the elevator, I asked Nikki what was up with all the pictures of babies in the cubicle across from her. She explained that the woman had been trying to get pregnant for over two years and was surrounding herself with babies to help her get pregnant. I started feeling bad for judging the baby photos and thinking she was crazy, but feeling bad didn't last long because Nikki asked, "So what the fuck is going on? What is so important that I had to leave work to talk to you? Did something happen in New York?"

"No, New York was awesome." The elevator got to the ground floor and Nikki and I made our way out of the building. I continued. "It has to do with Chase."

Nikki rolled her eyes as she said, "Oh, my fucking God! Audrey, get over him; he's such a douchebag."

"No, it's not that."

"Then what the fuck is it?"

"I accidentally sent my agent the story I wrote to get over Chase and she loved it. She wants to publish it and someone in Hollywood wants movie rights or some crap."

Nikki said, "Holy shit! Really?"

I said, "Yeah, I don't know what to do."

Nikki asked, "Does Chase know about this?"

"No, he doesn't even know I wrote the story."

"Dude, he's gonna be so pissed and jealous if you get a book deal and a movie deal after what happened with MTV."

I asked, "What happened with MTV?"

With hesitation, Nikki said, "Oh, shit. Bree and I agreed not to tell you because we didn't want you to think he'd get back together with you."

I asked, "Tell me what?"

"The reality show deal fell through with MTV."

I asked, "Really?"

"Don't get any fucking ideas."

Nikki and I walked into a restaurant and sat at the bar. I ordered a double vodka 7Up and Nikki ordered a Bloody Mary. It was only 11 a.m., but I needed to drink my woes away. After we ordered I asked, "What do you think I should do?"

"I say fuck him. Publish it and take the movie deal. I've never heard of a book so good that a movie deal gets in the works before the book is even published. That's ridiculous. When can I read it?"

"I'll email it to you, but should I ask Chase

his thoughts?"

Nikki asked, "Is it a fictional title or memoir?"

I said, "It's a memoir, but honestly, I just wanted the story to be scrap. I wrote it as scrap to get my feelings out, walk through my reality and fantasies with him, and then let it go."

"I understand what you are saying; if you publish it then you feel like you are holding on, but if you delete it then it's symbolic for letting go."

"Yeah, exactly. So what do I do?"

"Audrey, I honestly don't know. I guess I am going to have to read it to see."

Nikki and I sat at the bar for a few hours talking about the book and my amazing trip to New York. She actually had known all the details of what was going to happen because Ben had contacted her on Facebook. Since she had talked to Ben, I asked her what his deal was. She was also confused by it all, but said any girl would want a hot playboy millionaire turned nice guy who wants to settle down, so she wasn't sure why I didn't just marry him while I was there. I explained to her that I had just gotten out of a relationship and didn't need to jump into another relationship with some hot, rich guy I didn't know very well, but Nikki was convinced Ben was different.

After we were good and buzzed, we headed home and I sent Nikki a copy of my story, *Dating Chase Walker*. Nikki vowed to stay in and read it in its entirety. She said she'd stay up all night until she'd finished it. I decided it might be wise to read it again, too, before figuring out what the fuck I was going to do.

As I sipped on my wine, snuggled under a blanket on my couch reading the story, I felt uneasy in my stomach. It wasn't an uneasy sensation from the vodka mixing with the wine, but it was from reading words that brought my heart back to Chase. I didn't like it. I didn't want to read it again. I just wanted to delete the story and get back to moving on. I put my iPad down and decided I wasn't going to read it. I didn't want to walk through our whirlwind of a relationship again. I wasn't ready. I'd just wait and see what Nikki had to say and then go with her suggestion. She knew me better than anyone else and she had always been my number one supporter when it came to my writing.

Ben called to check on me. This guy was so nice and it confused me as to why he liked me. While Ben was telling me about his day, Nikki texted me saying, "YOU HAVE TO PUBLISH THIS" in all capital letters. Her next text said that she was only a few chapters in, but that she had never been able to connect with my words like she was at that moment.

I finished my conversation with Ben and then hung up the phone. I pulled my laptop off the coffee table and set it on my lap. While it was turning on, I decided I was going to check with Chase to see what he thought. Everyone was saying it was so great so maybe he'd be supportive of sharing it too. For a few minutes I thought about the words I'd use in an email to Chase letting him know that I was thinking about publishing the story I had written about our relationship. I wrote:

Dear Chase,

After we broke up I wrote this story as a way to let go of what we had. It got into the hands of some people and they'd like to publish it. I'd appreciate it if you would take some time over the next few days to read it and let me know what you think.

Best,
Audrey

TIME FOR AUDREY BUCHANAN

A few days passed and I had heard nothing from Chase. I decided I'd still allow for my publishers to start their end of the editing process. Not only did Nikki think it was my best writing, but Bree and my mom loved it. While I was at home working on articles for the RedEye newspaper, Wayne called. I picked up the phone and Wayne said, "Good afternoon, Audrey."

I said, "Hi, Wayne."

He asked, "Did you get all your stuff sorted out with Nikki last week?"

I said, "I did. I really appreciate you letting her leave early to help me sort things out."

"My pleasure; Nikki is a good worker."

"It really helped me to have her to talk to that day."

Wayne asked, "Is it something I can help with?"

I said, "No, it has to do with my ex and a memoir I think I am going to publish."

"Oh, I see. Well, Audrey, I sort of have an ulterior motive for calling. I did really want to check on you, but I also have a very strange question for you."

I hesitated as I said, "Okay, ask away."

Wayne said, "Next weekend I am going to Jamaica for a friend's wedding. I booked two tickets because at the time I was still engaged. I was just going to go by myself, but then I found out that everybody is bringing their girlfriend, fiancée, or wife. I will be the only person at the wedding without a significant other."

I interrupted Wayne a little and lightly said, "Okay."

"My ex-fiancée is going to be there with my old friend that she cheated on me with."

I said, "Ouch."

Wayne continued, "So I am just not up for going alone. Would you consider being my date for the weekend? All expenses paid and we will sleep in separate beds. You only have to pretend we are dating when we are around people."

Jokingly, I said, "Wayne, I'm not an escort."

Wayne sounded like he felt bad when he said, "Oh, no. I'm sorry, I didn't mean it like that at all."

I said, "I know, I'm kidding."

"Oh, okay. It's just if I showed up with a hot and fun city chick like you, it would make my ex-fiancée so jealous and the guys would think I was so cool. I know it all sounds childish, but you and I could have a great time. It sounds like you could use a vacation and I could really use the company."

I said, "Let me think about it."

Wayne asked, "Please? I'll buy you a whole new wardrobe for the weekend."

I said, "Wayne, you don't need to buy me clothes. If I go, it will be as friends and there will be no funny business."

Wayne said, "You have my word, Audrey."

The idea of getting away to Jamaica did sound perfect. I was hesitant on this whole thing because I really didn't know Wayne, but I figured since he was Nikki's boss he'd be on his best behavior. I decided to say fuck it and told Wayne I'd go with him to Jamaica. He was ecstatic and thanked me a hundred times.

The next week I packed my bags and I was off to Jamaica. Right after we checked into the resort, we put on our bathing suits to head down to the pool. When I walked out of the bathroom in my bikini Wayne said, "Audrey, you are beautiful. My ex-fiancée and friends are going to be so jealous!"

I laughed. We walked down to the pool and grabbed some towels and two chairs. I met a few of Wayne's old high school friends and then dipped into the pool to go chill at the swim-up bar. I preferred vodka, but rum was the liquor of Jamaica so I figured 'When in Rome...'. The bartender blended me up some fruity rum concoction and as I took my first sip I thought to myself how this was the perfect place to be right now. I wasn't sure how I'd managed to have two guys pay for two separate vacations in a matter of weeks, but whatever I was doing I hoped I'd keep doing it.

The girls at the resort for the wedding were pretty cliquey. When I was introduced to them, they held their hands out and said hello, but gave me looks like I disgusted them. I figured if I had to be around these girls for the next few days, I'd better try to make friends with them. While the guys were playing a very competitive game of volleyball in the pool, I walked over to a group of girls and said hello. They gave me snarky looks when I pulled up an empty chair next to them. That empty chair turned out to be a fucking hot seat and not a hot seat from sitting in the sun.

Since I'd been introduced to at least thirty people that afternoon, I couldn't remember any of the girls' names. I was too scared to ask for a name refresher because these girls did not look nice. As I quietly sipped on my fruity cocktail, feeling totally uncomfortable, I wished I had taken a few shots and gotten a better buzz going. Pregnant girl asked, "So, Audrey, how long have you and Wayne been dating?"

I said, "A little while."

Pig-nose girl butted in and asked, "Well, what's 'a little while?' Like, a couple of months?"

I said, "A few weeks."

Pig-nose girl continued, "You've only known Wayne for a few weeks and you came on vacation with him?"

I said, "Yes."

Pig-nose girl said, "That's weird."

I asked, "How is it weird?"

Pig-nose girl said, "It just is. Who would take a vacation with a guy she'd just met?"

I said, "I guess me."

Girl with the glitter flip flops, who you'd think I'd at least have remember her name because she was Wayne's ex-fiancé, asked, "What do you do for a living, Audrey?"

I hated the way these girls said my name, Audrey. It was so condescending. I said, "I'm a writer."

Pregnant girl jumped back in, requesting more detail, "What kind of writer?"

I said, "I'm an erotic romance novelist and I write for a local newspaper."

Pig-nose girl asked, "You write about sex?"

I said, "Yes, I write sexy stories."

Pig-nose girl said condescendingly, "Your father must be proud."

My God, these girls were bitches. I thought small town girls were supposed to be nice. I just said, "My father is very proud and supportive of what I do."

Pig-nose girl said, "Well, my father would disown me if I was doing something like that."

I said, "That's sad your father wouldn't support you following your dreams."

Pig-nose girl said, "It's not sad. It's staying respectful to my parents' name. What you do is as low as being a stripper."

What was with these girls? I had had enough. I simply said, "Lovely conversation, but I need to refill my drink. Do any of you need a refill?"

In unison, they all said, "No."

I said, "Okay, I'll see you tonight at the group dinner."

As I walked away I heard one girl say, "What a fucking whore."

My feelings were hurt, but why? I don't know. I knew these girls were bitchy, but I didn't understand why they didn't like me. I drank alone for a little while and then we went to dinner that night. None of the girls even noticed my existence at dinner. I felt myself latching on to Wayne for comfort. When we got back that night and we were lying in our separate beds, I asked Wayne why the girls didn't like me. Wayne said not to worry about it and that he'd take care of it.

The next day, Wayne and I went to Dunn's

River Falls for a few hours. We had fun, climbing the rocks and meeting new people who had no association with the wedding we were there for. These people were actually nice. That night we went out to dinner with a few other couples. The day of the wedding arrived and Wayne got up early to go golfing with all the guys. I slept in a bit and then headed downstairs with my iPad to do some reading while I ate breakfast. I spotted pregnant girl, glitter flip flop girl, pig-nose girl and some other girls. I stood up and walked over to them. I said, "Hey, I have a table and there's an open one next to it. Want to pull them together so we can all eat together?"

Pig-nose girl said, "Fuck off, you whore. You are a tattletale and said we were being mean to you. Fuck you, you haven't seen mean yet." Then pig-nose girl walked past me, intentionally nudging me with her shoulder. The girls all followed behind her, giving me nasty looks as they passed by me. I felt tears coming on, like a big ugly cry was about to explode out of my face. I walked over to my table and grabbed my iPad then rushed back to my room, laid down on the bed, and began to weep. These girls didn't deserve my tears, but I felt like I had been brought back to high school where girls would constantly torture me. After my big-ass ugly cry was over, I walked outside and sat on the balcony. I had to let my red eyes tone down a bit before anyone could see me.

As I was sitting taking in the beautiful view, the old guy on the balcony next to mine asked, "Is everything alright?"

I said, "Yes, just taking in the view."

He asked, "Beautiful, isn't it?"

I said, "It's amazing."

Old guy then asked, "Want to get high? The view will look even better."

Did this old gray-haired dude really just ask me if I wanted to get high? I needed confirmation that I'd heard him correctly. I asked, "What?"

"Come over to my balcony and get high with me. The weed here is amazing."

Even though my father was a huge stoner, I'd never smoked. I had tried it back in the day, but always preferred liquor. I figured, what the fuck, I was on vacation; so I crawled over the balcony and smoked a joint with the old dude. As we were smoking, I told him the story about why I was crying. After I was high, I told him the story about publishing my memoir. Because he was way stoned, his advice was long and deep, but the gist of it was that he thought I should publish it. He said that stories and art are meant to be shared so they can inspire others.

Our long conversation was great, but I started to get the munchies. I said, "I'm hungry."

The old guy said, "Me too. Let's go get one of those jerk chicken sandwiches. They are amazing."

I said, "Okay." As we were walking I realized we hadn't introduced ourselves yet so I said, "My name is Audrey, by the way."

Old guy said, "Nice to meet you, Audrey. I'm Earl."

Earl and I ate our jerk chicken sandwiches and chatted for a while longer. As we were walking back to our rooms, I spotted glitter flip flop girl and she walked up to us like she was pissed off. Glitter flip flop girl said, "Dad, what are you doing with this girl?"

Earl said, "Tonya, just grabbed some sandwiches together."

Tonya! That was Wayne's ex-fiancé's name! Tonya, also known as glitter flip flop girl, grabbed Earl's hand and said, "Stay away from this whore, Dad. Let's go."

Earl sort of rolled his eyes as glitter flip flop girl dragged him away. He yelled out, "Very nice to meet you, Audrey. Have a good day."

I got back to the room and while I was taking a shit, I heard Wayne walk into our room. I pushed my poop out fast, flushed the toilet, and sprayed some hairspray to try to cover up the smell. I walked out of the bathroom and said hi to Wayne. He suggested we to go to the pool for a couple hours before the wedding and I agreed.

That night at the wedding Wayne was extra sweet to me. I think he could sense I was feeling uncomfortable being around the mean girls. We drank a lot, danced, and then took a long walk on the beach. When we got back to the room, my drunk self thought how this guy had been really nice to me and that maybe I should give him a blowjob to thank him. Sounds whoreish, but I was feeling sexy in my dress and I wanted to do something nice for Wayne. I kissed him and then undressed him. He was a light lip kisser, which was nice. Nothing is worse than a guy who sticks his tongue down your throat and tries to eat your last meal.

Once his shirt was off, I worked my lips

down his stomach and unbuttoned his pants. I let them drop to the floor and then I pulled down his underwear. I looked at his cock and my eyes widened. I was in shock. I didn't know what to do. He had dirty blonde pubic hair that was insanely long and out of control. It was disgustingly bad. He needed a pubic hair hairbrush to mane that mess. And his cock, oh his cock. I don't think I could even call it a cock. It was so small I think it would have to be classified as a peenie. Poor Wayne! That's some serious bad luck.

There was no turning back, though. What would I say? Your peenie is so small that I don't know how to find it in your bush and give it a blowjob? I had to proceed. I put his itty bitty cock in my mouth and moved it in and out. I heard Wayne moan in pleasure, while I was kneeling on the ground in pain trying not to sneeze because his pubic hairs were tickling my nose so bad. Luckily, Wayne didn't last long before he came in my mouth.

I swallowed his cum and then went to the bathroom to brush my teeth and put my pajamas on while he recovered from his orgasm on the bed. When I came out of the bathroom Wayne said, "I forgot how amazing blowjobs are. I haven't had one in, like, five years."

I said, "Really - five years? Are you exaggerating?"

Wayne said, "No, my ex-fiancée didn't like giving blowjobs."

I said, "That sucks. Good thing you didn't marry her. A lifetime with no blowjobs would suck."

TIME FOR AUDREY BUCHANAN

I got back from Jamaica and I still hadn't received a response from Chase regarding the story I'd sent him. The publishers finished their final edits and they wanted to move forward to have the book on the shelves before Christmas. I hadn't agreed to publish it because I hadn't talked to Chase yet, but they had everything ready to go. I decided to send a follow-up email to Chase:

Dear Chase,
Have you had a chance to look at my story yet? My publisher wants to move forward so we can have it on shelves for holiday buyers. It's important that you are on board before I move forward.
Best,
Audrey

I pressed send and a few minutes later I got a response:

I read a couple of pages, but I don't have time to be reading your stuff right now. Do whatever you want to do, Audrey. I don't care.

Sent from my iPhone

I felt my heart hurt a little. He didn't have time? Inside I knew I really just wanted to burn or delete the story to let Chase go, but I was torn because I wanted to be able to share such an emotional human experience. I decided to call Ben and ask his advice. Ben didn't answer, but called me back a few minutes later. He said he was just leaving dinner. After he told me all about his amazing dinner I said, "Ben, can I ask you something?"

Ben said, "Of course, darling, what's up?"

"What do you think I should do about publishing this memoir?"

Ben asked, "Did your ex ever email you back?"

I said, "He just did. He said he doesn't have time to read my stuff and he doesn't care."

"Ouch. I think the only thing you can do is separate yourself from your emotions with this one. If you look at it as a story instead of a personal experience then it might be easier to share it."

"I know you are right, but how do I just let it go so easily?"

Ben said, "Appreciate what you had and realize it is just a memory. Let go of that fantasy in your head that is making you hold on. You are still holding onto something that makes you think you guys will get back together. If you weren't, you could let the story go around the world a million times without a worry. You don't want to be with this guy. I say this because you deserve better and because, like all guys, I have an ulterior motive and would love for you to move on so I can have a chance to sweep you off your feet."

I laughed as I said, "All guys have ulterior motives, but your advice is really good. Why are you so nice to me?"

"I already told you; I like you. I was an idiot, so focused on work when I first met you, but now I'm ready to give you the best me."

I teased Ben by saying, "You are crazy."

"When I met you, there was just something about you, but I was so caught up in making money. Now that I've made plenty and I got to spend some time with you I know I'd like to give us a shot."

Ben and I talked a little bit longer; just talking with him made me feel better. After we hung up the phone, I sat down in front of my laptop and opened the final edited copy of *Dating Chase Walker* that my publishers had sent me. I stared at it for several minutes and then decided to respond to the email from my agent, letting her know I was ready to move forward. It was time for me to let Chase go and deleting the story would make things easier, but allowing it to be published would be my way of appreciating what we had and the inspiration he had given me.

I had avoided life and Chicago for several weeks, but it was time I got myself back out and about. I had no desire to date and, if I did, I'd be giving Ben the first chance. I'd relied on Chase for inspiration with my last few books so now it was time to find it within myself, time to love myself, and time just to worry about me.

For the next couple of weeks I went out - a lot. I had fun, I drank and I danced. Getting myself out gave me a sense of confidence. I still thought about Chase a lot. I didn't want to, but it seemed like everything reminded me of him. From songs on my Pandora radio, to clothes he had bought me, to eating pizza that was cut into squares – his pet peeve - instead of pie-cut. I powered through all the reminders though, and each time he popped into my mind, I tried to think of something else. Similar to how guys think of baseball during sex.

On a Saturday afternoon, Bree texted me asking if I'd go to an event her boyfriend, Scotty Stylez, was promoting. Like I had done for every event she'd tried to get me to go in the past few weeks, I responded by asking if Chase would be there. She replied that it was highly unlikely, so I said I was in. Bree picked me up in a cab and we headed over to American Junkie. There was a line outside, but we were able to finagle our way in without waiting. When we got inside, we ordered drinks and walked around saying hi to industry people we knew. I had my eyes open for cute guys to flirt with, but I was still in no mood for men. DJ Dante the Don was playing some good music so once I had a buzz I told Bree we should go to the front and dance, but she wasn't up for it. I told her I was going to dance without her then. I worked my way to the front near the stage and found a couple of girls who drunkenly invited me in to dance with them.

They each introduced themselves, but it was so loud that I didn't catch their names. It really didn't matter because I was never any good at remembering names. After a lot of dancing and lemon drop shots, one of the girls said their group was heading out to go to The Underground. They asked if I wanted to go with them. I found Bree and asked if she wanted to go to The Underground, but she said she was ready to go home to go to bed; a standard response for a girl in a relationship. I told her I was going to head over to The Underground with a group of girls that I had just met. Bree gave me a hug goodbye while she told me to have fun, but be safe.

My new girlfriends and I walked down the street in our heels in the chilly fall air and luckily didn't have to wait in line at The Underground because I was starting to feel really cold. When we got inside, I followed the group of girls because they said they were meeting people there and I had no idea who the people were that they were meeting. They found the people they were looking for at a table and they had the bottle service girl pour us all drinks. Once I had my drink, I took a seat next to one of the girls I'd met. I moved in close to her and said, "I'm sorry, I can't remember your name."

The girl responded, "I'm Lizzette. Your name is Audrey, right?"

I said, "Yes."

Lizzette said, "Want to chug these drinks and go dance?"

I said, "Sure."

We chugged down our drinks and then went to the front to dance. While I was dancing, I realized that last drink *had* to be my last. I felt good, but one more and I wouldn't be able to stand. We were having fun dancing, but then Lizzette started getting touchy-feely. She was grinding up on me and the guys around us were starting to notice. She was hot, but I had never danced like this with a woman before. I decided to roll with it and grinded on her right back. I figured we were drunk girls having fun.

Lizzette moved in close to me and said, "I have to pee. Let's go to the bathroom."

I nodded my head up and down in response, letting her know I needed to pee too. Lizzette grabbed my hand and led me to the bathroom. I didn't think anything of it because Nikki and I held hands sometimes when we were trying to weave our way through a crowded club. When we got into the bathroom, we stood in line. While we were waiting, Lizzette said, "I am having so much fun with you. Let's hang out this week."

I figured it was just drunk girl-talk and that I'd never actually see her again, but being a girl, I said, "Oh, my God! Yes, we have to hang out again."

We got to the front of the bathroom line and Lizzette grabbed my hand again. She said, "Come into the stall with me."

I said, "The bathroom stalls are small. I'll wait for the next one. You go."

Lizzette said, "No, come with me."

I followed Lizzette's lead and once we got into the stall she pushed me up against the wall and kissed me with aggression. I kissed her back while thinking: *Fuck - what is going on here*? I had never hooked up with a girl before. Maybe she was just drunk and having fun? Or was she gay? Maybe bisexual? As she continued to kiss me, her hands moved around my chest, grabbing my boobs. I started feeling a little turned on. What the hell was going on? I had never hooked up with a woman and here I was in a club bathroom getting felt up by a random girl and I was turned on. I couldn't decide if I should let this go further and enjoy it or run the fuck out of the bathroom stall. Luckily, the bathroom attendant decided for us when she knocked on our stall and said, "Girls, hurry up!"

We walked out of the stall without having a chance to pee. I stopped to wash my hands, but Lizzette didn't. Gross. We walked out of the bathroom and I told Lizzette I needed to head home. She said, "No, don't go. My boyfriend is probably here now. I want you to meet him."

This girl had a boyfriend? What the hell was going on? I was confused. I needed to get out of this place. I said, "I'm sorry, I need to head home."

Lizzette said, "Okay, but put your number in my phone so we can hang out soon."

I put my phone number in Lizzette's phone and then she gave me a light kiss on the lips before I headed out. I felt like everyone at the club was staring at us. When I got upstairs, I hailed a cab. On the ride home I called Nikki, but she didn't answer. I called Bree too, but no answer. Fuck, what just happened? I'd just made out with a girl and liked it. Had my break-up with Chase hurt me so bad that I had turned gay?

When I got home, I couldn't stop thinking about my make-out session with Lizzette. This girl had a boyfriend, but she made out with me. Is screwing around with the same sex while in a relationship with the opposite sex okay? The situation raised so many questions in my head, but mostly I wondered why I had been turned on by Lizzette. I decided to take the experience and utilize it to see if it could get me off.

I went into the bathroom and took off my make-up before brushing my teeth. I came out of the bathroom and undressed, but before I put my pajamas on I lay down on my bed and let my imagination run wild. I thought about Lizzette and the small bathroom stall we'd been in when she pushed me up against the wall and she put her lips on mine. I slowly rubbed my clit, imagining her lips on mine and her hands caressing my breasts. I felt my pussy start to get wet. My imagination went further and I imagined Lizzette pulling my dress off over my head while I stood with my bare breasts out, only wearing panties. Once my dress was off, we kissed more passionately while her hand rubbed my clit through my panties.

I moved things further in my head and slipped her dress off. I looked at her naked bare body, small breasts, and hard nipples. I moved my mouth from kissing her lips down her chest to licking her nipples. From there I moved further down, pulling her panties off and seeing her pussy. I used my tongue and licked it gently. I began to moan, thinking about my tongue on her pussy. In reality, I wouldn't know what to do to get a girl off with my tongue, but in my fantasy I was doing everything right. In my fantasy I could hear her moaning in pleasure while I was moaning out loud from my fantasy. I could also feel her body tightening up in pleasure and telling me I was doing a good job.

I moved my fantasy to her taking control of my body. She kissed my lips lightly and moved her fingers over my clit. As I rubbed my own clit, I pretended they were her fingers. I moved them faster and faster, feeling myself get more wet with each motion until the pleasure was so intense that my body tensed up and I orgasmed with a loud moan. I pulled my blanket over me and fell asleep naked. I felt so relaxed that I didn't even want to get up to put my pajamas on.

I woke up in the morning to my phone ringing out in my living room. I knew it was Nikki from the ringtone so I ignored it, but she kept calling back. After the fourth time, I decided to get up and find my phone. When I was getting up, I noticed a big dry cum stain on my bed and the first thing that crossed my mind was that it was about time.

I answered the phone and Nikki didn't even say hello; instead, she blurted out, "Is everything okay?"

I said, "Yeah, I'm fine. Why?"

Nikki asked, "Why did you call me in the middle of the night?"

I asked, "Have you ever had sex with a girl?"

Nikki responded, "Yeah, a few times. You know that."

"Like full-on sex?"

"Only once with just me and a girl. The other times were part of a threesome. You know this, so why did you call me in the middle of the night? Were you writing something?"

"No. I made out with a girl in a bathroom stall last night."

"Shut the fuck up! You finally made the move. It's about time."

"Actually, this girl named Lizzette made the move, and why do you say 'finally?'"

"You are the most sexually curious person I know, yet you are such a prude."

"I am no prude."

"Yes, you are. You love writing about sex, but you don't explore bondage and you've never been with a woman, let alone taken part in a threesome."

"That doesn't make me a prude. I'm getting there."

Nikki asked, "So, how far did you go with this girl?"

I said, "We just made out and felt each other's boobs. She wanted me to meet her boyfriend, but I ran away like a chicken. I ended up coming home and masturbating thinking of our encounter."

Nikki asked, "And?"

I said, "And it was good. I gave her my number so I am thinking if she calls I might meet up with her and see what happens. She might've just been drunk though."

"No, if she wanted you to meet her boyfriend then she was trying to pull you for a threesome."

I asked, "Really?"

"Yeah! Do you know how many couples have tried to pull me in for a threesome? I think you should do it. Threesomes can be a lot of fun."

I asked, "Wouldn't a one-on-one with a girl be better to do first?"

"No way! Threesomes are far less intimidating."

"I guess I have a lot to think about. I feel

like I am only wanting to get with a girl because I knew Chase really wanted us to have a threesome. That my sudden intrigue was only there because if I did it, maybe he'd want me back."

"Audrey, you are a fucking idiot. Even if he wanted you back, I wouldn't allow you to get back with him."

I asked, "You wouldn't allow it?"

Nikki said, "Fuck, no. I could kick your ass any day so if he ever tried I'd restrain you."

I said, "I guess that's one of the many reasons I love you, Nikki."

few days later, there had been no call or text from Lizzette so I figured it had been just a drunken incident for her. I Googled threesomes quite a bit because the incident had left me feeling intrigued. I started to think that maybe it was time for me to experience sex with a woman, even if there was a little bit of an ulterior motive behind it. Even Nikki supported me in trying it out and what could it hurt to try? I knew I wasn't looking for a relationship with a girl; I just wanted to try one on for size. While I was browsing lesbian porn on YouPorn.com, I heard a knock on my door. I turned the volume down and closed my computer quickly, worried that the person on the other side of the door might have heard the moaning from the porno I'd been watching. When I stood up to go answer the door, I felt that my panties were a little wet. I opened the door and my agent was on the other side. She held up a book that had the title *Dating Chase Walker* on it. She said, "Here's the first copy of your book."

I asked, "Why are you hand delivering it?"

My agent said, "Clear your schedule. Don't eat, don't drink, don't even sleep. Read through this book tonight and as soon as you finish, let me know. It's ready to start printing in bulk as soon as we give the okay."

I said, "Wait, this is happening so fast."

"Audrey, I told you we wanted it out for the holiday buyers. I got you a public relations agent, too. He is in the process of putting together a book launch party for you. You will meet with him in a few days. He's going to be filling your schedule with interviews and events, so keep your schedule free from personal activities."

"Whoa, whoa, this is really fucking fast."

"The next few months, probably even longer, of your life are going to be a whirlwind. This book is going to be a bestseller."

I asked, "How do you know that it will be a bestseller?"

"I've been doing this for years and I know a lot of people who have been doing this for years. Every person who has read this book has said the same thing."

I asked, "What happens if it doesn't end up being one?"

My agent said with sass, "Audrey, are you questioning whether I know how to do my job?"

I said, "No, no. I just worry that if all this money and time goes into it, then what happens if people don't like my story?"

"They will. Now take this book and read it. Call me the second you are finished. I'll be setting up meetings for this week with your new PR agent and on Friday the producer and script writers are flying in from Los Angeles."

I asked, "Wait, why are we already starting to work on the movie?"

"Audrey, do you have any idea how long it takes to script, cast, and produce a movie? Most take years. They want to start talking numbers this Friday so you should probably bring your lawyer with you."

"Wait, my lawyer specializes in literary contracts. Would he be good for this?"

My agent said, "No, get yourself the best entertainment lawyer you can find. I can connect you with some if you need me to."

I took a deep breath and then said, "This is a lot to take in."

"Get used to it. Now go read the book and remember to call me as soon as you finish reading it. You hear me? As soon as you finish it!"

"Okay, okay, I will."

My agent left and I sat down on my couch holding the printed and bound copy of *Dating Chase Walker*. I wasn't excited to read it. I started thinking about when I got the first book in my book series sent to me and I was so excited reading it. I couldn't wait for Chase to come home so I could show him. With this book, I wasn't excited in the least bit and honestly I had zero desire to share it with anyone I knew. *Fuck, was it too late to turn back?*

I read through each page, feeling so much emotion inside and wishing that I had Chase there to read it with me and encourage me to continue publishing it. I wanted him there to let me know that my story and my art were okay to share. I wanted to love the story and love the emotion behind it, but I just kept getting angry with myself for allowing it to make me miss Chase. I took a break and poured myself a glass of wine. While I was pouring my wine, I thought about Ben's advice to let go of my emotion for Chase. How could I do that? How could I get rid of it while reading the words I'd written because of emotion? I decided I'd try reading it, making Chase into a fictional character. I physically designed a fictional man in my head so every time I read his name and every scenario I was reading I'd see this fictional man instead of Chase. It actually helped and with each chapter I finished I was enjoying reading the story a little more.

When I got to the Kelly incident – the girl he felt he needed to game while we were together - I felt pain inside me. I didn't want to be reliving the pain of his betrayal with Kelly, the pain of our trip to Mexico, and the pain of the moment when I'd written the last paragraph in the book. I powered through, though. Reliving and feeling that pain might actually lead me to truly let go. I had written *Dating Chase Walker* as a way to let go, but I hadn't fully let go. I wasn't a miracle worker; I knew it would take time. Healing from love, even one-sided love, takes time.

I stayed up all night reading the story, as my agent had said I should. I sent her a text at 4:48am saying I was finished and I'd be sending a few minor edits via email. After I'd sent the edits, I crawled into bed and cried myself to sleep. Writing a memoir of love was an emotional rollercoaster, but reading that memoir of love after you've so badly wanted to let it go was a mind-fuck.

When I woke up, there was a text from my agent saying that my book had been sent off to print. I cried again. What was I doing? Allowing my relationship to be exposed to the world, allowing a man's life to be exposed without him caring, and allowing my deepest personal emotions to be felt by any and everybody who wanted to read my work. I needed the support of my mom and dad so I called my mom. She answered with a question, "Audrey, you finally have time for your mother?"

I blurted out in tears, along with what sounded like an uncomfortable breath, "Mommy."

My mom responded, "Oh, shit, you said 'Mommy.' Audrey, what is wrong?"

I said, while continuing my cry, "I don't know what I am getting myself into! I'm so scared, but so excited at the same time."

My mom asked, "What did you get yourself into?"

"Mom, this memoir; it's going to be the death of me."

My mom said, "Oh, Audrey, quit being dramatic. You are just emotional because you expected Chase to support you and be on board, but he's completely ignored it all. He'll come around and will man up and read it at some point. It is a perfect story that will inspire and turn on a lot of women and men."

I laughed as I said, "Mom, gross! Don't say it is going to turn people on. You shouldn't think that."

"It will. The way you exposed your sex life with him was beautiful."

"Oh my God, Mom, stop."

"Alright, I'll stop, if you stop crying."

My mom telling me to stop crying made me start crying again and I said, "But, Mom!"

She responded, "I said stop crying, or I am going to keep talking about your sex life."

I took a deep breath and said, "Fine."

"Good. Now clean your act up and come out here for the night. I'll make dinner, we'll drink wine and I'll even hurry over to the bakery before it closes to buy you some of those apple cider donuts that you love."

"I do love those donuts."

"And you love us, too. So get your act together, shower, and then come and hang out with us for the night. We miss our little girl."

I did as my mom instructed and got my shit together before I left. I walked down the street to find my car; I literally hadn't driven my car in a month so I'd forgotten where I'd parked the old thing. Of course, when I walked up to my car it had three parking tickets on the windshield; fucking Chicago and their meter maids, always ticketing for ridiculous reasons. I got into my car and after three attempts, the baby finally started up. As I worked my way out of the super-tight parking spot I was in, I decided that if I really did get a movie deal I was going to buy myself an expensive and insanely unnecessary car; maybe a Bentley or Maserati. Whatever I bought, it had to be ridiculous.

I arrived at my parents' and my mom welcomed me with a hug, a donut, and a glass of wine. I already felt comforted. We sat down in the living room while we waited for my father. I ate my donut while she updated me on what my aunts, uncles, cousins, and grandma were up to. It was a good distraction from my spinning mind. I got relaxed and comfortable and as soon as my father got home from work, my mom went into the kitchen. My father sat down in his old smelly recliner chair with a pile of mail.

Some things never changed. He half paid attention to me while he was sorting through the mail, but once he had read it all he put it on the side table and asked, "So, to what do we owe the pleasure of this visit?"

I said, "Mom said I needed some mom-and-dad time."

My dad said, "Oh," before he stood up, opened his arms and welcomed me in for a hug. I began to cry again. As he hugged me, he asked, "What's got you down, little bug?"

I said, "Dad, I am living a writer's dream right now, but hating every moment of it."

"Why would you hate what your mother says is your most beautiful creation?"

"Because I feel sneaky, I feel wrong, and I feel bad exposing this story without the support of Chase."

"Audrey, you have to let it go. The only reason you are feeling bad is because you don't want to hurt him and you are still in love with him."

I said with a little attitude, "Don't remind me, Dad."

"Hey, I don't blame you for still loving him. Love is divine so who would want to let it go? When you truly let him go, there will be no worries in you. It will be seen as what you intended it to be; a love and sex story so good that it's meant to live on through the written word."

My mother yelled from the kitchen, "Listen to your father, Audrey, he always gives good advice."

Feeling like my mother had ruined the moment, I yelled back, "I know, Mom."

Our dinner talk was all about me. It was fantastic. Their consensus was that I should move forward with publishing the memoir and that I had made the right decision. It was my memory of the relationship we had. It was my fantasy that I had put into words, not his, so I didn't need him on board. We also talked about Ben and my mother told me to convince Ben to move to Chicago and marry him, but my father's advice was the one I knew I had to take. He said, "Audrey, jumping into another relationship is not wise. Enjoy the next few months of your career and take time for Audrey Buchanan. If you focus on loving you then you will be able to let go of Chase and let someone else in."

I asked, "What happens if I miss my chance with Ben though?"

My father replied, "That means it wasn't meant to be. This guy came out of nowhere looking to suddenly settle down. I think he needs a couple of months to make sure he is truly wanting what he says he wants."

I said, "That's true."

My dad asked, "So, what are you going to do these next few months?"

I said, "Umm..."

He said, "Oh, come on, now."

I laughed, because my dad always had to end lessons with exciting recaps. I said with enthusiasm, "I am going to take time for Audrey Buchanan!"

The next morning I had breakfast with my father and he briefed me on all things legal. He called his friend, my literary contract lawyer, and told him everything I needed. He called another friend of his who was an entertainment lawyer and briefed him on the meeting that was scheduled for Friday with the producer and script writer. Even though I wasn't much of a logistical person, I felt a lot better about the whole thing once my father had helped me to understand and get everything in order. I drove back to the city that day with confidence and excitement, thinking about how it was time for me, Audrey Buchanan.

TIME FOR AUDREY BUCHANAN

Friday, the big day of meetings, arrived. I was nervous, so I was up extra early. I ate a couple of donuts and headed out the door. On the way to my agent's office, my mother texted me to make sure I was awake and dressed nicely. Apparently, I have yet to prove to my parents that I can be a responsible adult. As I was about to respond to my mother's text, Ben called to wish me luck. Ben would qualify as a responsible adult, so why he had a thing for me was beyond me. When the cab pulled up in front of my agent's office, I got a text from my agent saying they were running a half-hour late. Of course, the one time I'm early would be the one time my agent is late. I said to Ben, "My agent is running late."

Ben responded, "Go get yourself a mimosa; it'll calm your nerves."

At that moment, I felt love for this man. What a brilliant idea. I told the cabbie to drive down the street to a restaurant that served brunch. I said goodbye to Ben and then paid the cabbie before getting out and walking into the restaurant. As I was walking in the restaurant, my mother called me and when I answered she yelled into the phone, "Audrey, are you awake?"

I said, "Yes, Mom, I am walking into a restaurant."

My mother said, "I thought you were meeting at your agent's office."

"We are, but they are running late so I am going to get a mimosa."

"You shouldn't walk into a meeting smelling like alcohol."

I asked, "Why not?"

My mother responded, "It's unprofessional. Don't drink before the meeting."

I said, "But, Mom..."

"No 'but's.'"

"But I'm so nervous."

"No 'but's', Audrey! You are meeting with agents, public relations professionals, lawyers, a producer, and who knows who else today. You need to be sober."

"Mom, I won't get drunk off one mimosa."

"Go to the office. Be punctual. Be professional."

"Alright, Mom, I promise I will consider all the things you just said."

"Oh Christ, Audrey, I know what that means. Fine, drink a mimosa, but eat some mints before the meeting for crying out loud."

I said, "I love you, Mom."

She responded, "I love you, too. Good luck today and call me when you can."

I sat down at the bar in the restaurant and took the mimosa down like a champ. I ordered a second and decided to share with the bartender my day ahead. Once the second mimosa was in my belly, I popped a few mints in my mouth which the bartender had so kindly provided for me. As I walked away, he wished me luck. I walked down the street feeling good and ready. I loved how a little champagne, wine, vodka, or any alcohol could make me relax so easily. I walked into my agent's office and she still hadn't arrived so her assistant instructed me to sit and wait. I browsed Facebook to kill time until my agent walked in with a very attractive man. As my agent was walking by me in a hurry, she said, "Audrey, follow us."

I stood up quickly and followed them into her office. As my agent was putting her stuff on her desk, the very attractive man introduced himself, "Hi, Audrey, I'm Steven, your new PR agent."

The moment he began talking I thought: *Damn, this hot guy is gay. All the really hot ones are.* I said, "Hi, Steven, I'm looking forward to working with you."

My agent cut in and said, "Steven knows what he's doing. Never question what he tells you to do, just do it."

I said, "Okay."

Steven said, "Don't worry, darling, I'm not as big of a fireball as her."

I smiled at Steven as I sat down and waited for a million things to start coming at me. And boy, was I right. Steven had every day planned out for me for the next month. I expected that maybe I'd see an agenda of some sort, but the document he handed me was insane. It had every single day planned out for me for the next month. I asked, "Are these the things I get to pick from to do?"

Steven said, "No, darling, you are doing all of this."

I asked, "How?"

"Just follow my lead."

"You realize that Thanksgiving is in less

than two weeks."

My agent said, "Why do you think we are rushing all this? We want those holiday buyers. We want your book to top the lists right away."

Steven said, "Don't plan to sleep until next year. I am going to keep you tremendously busy with promotions."

My agent said, "Your book is going to be flying off the shelves. Everybody is going to want a copy for Christmas."

I asked, "How are stores going to have copies so fast?"

My agent said, "They start shipping out Monday. Now, no more questions; just listen to Steven."

I shut up, sat back, and let Steven talk my ear off while I half listened. After he was finished jabbering about who knows what - I wasn't really paying attention - he said, "Audrey, open up the schedule."

I did as instructed and saw the schedule started bright and early Monday morning with a fitting at the posh Chicago boutique, Akira. I got excited and asked, "Do I get an outfit from Akira to wear?"

Steven said, "They are your sponsor. From now on, you do not attend any media - wait - do not even leave the house unless you are wearing Akira. Each week they will provide you with new clothing and if anyone ever asks you what you are wearing, you say Akira."

I said, "Got it, only Akira. That's a pretty sweet deal. Can I get a wine and donut sponsor, too?"

Steven looked at me funny and then let out a little laugh as he said, "Oh, that's cute. You made a joke."

I actually wasn't joking, but I didn't have time to tell him that because he moved on to the next item on the list: a photo shoot. From there, it was on to the "exclusive" book launch event at Hotel 71. I asked who was going to be invited and Steven said the best of the best in Chicago. I asked if my parents could come and he said he could add them to the list. *He could add my parents to the list?* They should be the first fucking people on the list. After the book launch it was interview, interview, interview, Thanksgiving, interview, interview - I think you get it. I'd be traveling from New York to Los Angeles to Miami and then back to New York. I'd literally be traveling from Thanksgiving until Christmas. *What the hell had I gotten myself into?*

After the schedule review, Steven and I did a practice interview. I failed. We did another one and I failed again. I finally said, "Steven, just tell me what I need to say when I go into these and I'll say it."

Steven said, "Audrey, I can't just tell you what to say. I need you to talk with the same emotion as in your book. Get people hooked and let them feel what you are feeling."

I said, "Umm, Steven, you realize that I wrote that book with intense emotion and boogers running out of my nose. I don't think that kind of state would be appropriate for interviews."

Steven responded, "I'm not being literal. I'm saying you need to reveal why you fell for this guy and why they need to read the book and experience the whirlwind sexual love affair you two had. Why you chose to share this book with others."

"I didn't choose to share this story. Okay, technically, yes, I did make the decision, but I wrote this story to get over a dude. It got in the hands of that lady over there," I pointed to my agent, "And she was the one who got so inspired by it."

My agent cut in, "I know great writing when I see it and I wasn't the only one inspired by it."

Steven said, "Alright, you two, let's move on. Audrey, get in touch with those feelings you felt right after this guy broke your heart and bring that into the interviews."

"Fuck that, Steven. Do you realize how hard I am working to get over Chase Walker? Now you want me to put myself back in that place? No way. I refuse."

With some attitude, Steven said, "Well, then, I am just going to have to make it happen."

I asked, "What's that supposed to mean?"

"Don't you worry your pretty little face. Now let's move on. I need you to fill out this questionnaire."

I asked, "What's it for?"

"For the greenrooms before your interviews. They take requests on what people want while they are waiting to go on air."

I said, "I'm simple. All I need is a donut with champagne, wine, or vodka to wash it down."

"What kind of donut? What kind of champagne? Fill out the questionnaire."

I filled out the questionnaire and then we left the office for a tasting at Hotel 71. After the tasting, I was free to take a break. I went home stuffed and took a nap. I woke up to Ben calling. I answered with a groggy, "Hello."

Ben said with excitement on the other end of the line, "So, how did it all go?"

I said, "It was boring and a lot of work."

Ben asked, "Did you get a movie deal?"

"That meeting is tonight, I guess. My bossy book agent and overwhelming PR agent let me come home for a few hours to nap."

"They should; you are the talent."

I said, "I am not the talent. I'm just a writer."

"Never say that you are just a writer. You are a writer who connected with some serious emotions and somehow put those emotions into the written word. You are going to connect with and inspire millions."

I asked, "How so? I wrote about sex, love, and timing."

Ben said, "People read, people watch talk shows, people watch movies because they want to connect and be reminded that they are not alone. Women and men are going to want to feel all the good and bad things you went through with Chase. Considering that I am crushing on you big-time, I'm scared to read the book, but I do think you should connect and expose yourself from where you are at. It's important. Tell them you fell in love, believed in it, and got your heart broken, but now you are doing just fine. Yes, you struggle some days, but you've come a long way."

I asked, "How do you know I struggle?"

With seriousness, Ben said, "Audrey, you started crying when we were about to have sex." I laughed, but Ben said, "Don't laugh."

I said, "I'm sorry. I'd almost forgotten about that. I'm still embarrassed."

Ben said, "Don't be."

"I still don't understand why you are still sticking around."

"Audrey, I keep asking myself why I suddenly started mad crushing on you too, but I can't seem to answer that for myself."

I said, "Well, Mr. Crusher, want to be my date to my fancy schmancy invite-only book launch party next Saturday?"

Ben said, "Oh, what have I gotten myself into?"

"Is that a no, Ben? Apparently, I have enough money to afford a PR agent now so I can buy your plane ticket."

"Audrey, you know I have more than enough money. I'm saying that I am crushing on a girl who wrote a book about being in love and having fantastic sex with her ex-boyfriend; an ex-boyfriend whom she hasn't gotten over yet. Now I am going to fly to be her date to the book launch for the book she wrote about her love for him and their fantastic sex."

"Yeah, that shit's out of control. You might want to back away from me. Go join ChristianSingles.com or at least EHarmony.com. They at least pre-screen the bitches on there. I'd probably get rejected."

"I don't need those sites. I picked you up on Facebook."

"You picked me up on a yacht when you were shitfaced from drinking all day in the sun."

"Yeah, that story is way cooler and less

creepy than the Facebook pick-up story. So, what do I need to know about the book launch? When should I fly in? What should I wear? And is Chase going to be there?"

My stomach dropped a little. *Shit, would Chase be at the book launch? I didn't know.* I said, "I don't know the answer to any of those. Let me shower and go to this dinner. I'll get more details and call you tomorrow."

"Sounds good. Good luck tonight and if you are unsure about anything, do not sign on the dotted line!"

Ben sounded just like my father. I jokingly said, "Thanks, Dad."

"Have a good night, Audrey."

"You too, Ben."

I got out of bed, took a shower and got ready. While I was dancing around my apartment to "Diddy" by Paperboy, I heard my phone ringing. It was my dad. I answered and he asked, "Audrey, are you all ready for your meeting tonight?"

I said, "Yes, I am, but I thought it was this afternoon."

My father said, "I knew you wouldn't have your ducks in a row that's why I put Phil in direct contact with your agent."

I said, "Oh, glad you have faith in me."

"I very much do, but when it comes to planning, well, it's just not your thing."

"Yeah, yeah. So, Dad..."

"Yes, Audrey."

"Are you sure I am making the right decision moving forward with all this?"

"Well, Audrey dear, I believe that you wrote a story from the heart; a story that many will be touched by. I believe you truly want people to read that story. The thing is you have to play the media game if you want more people to read your story, but you are scared of the media. This is all brand new to you. Sure, you've done little promotional things here and there, but this is much bigger."

I said, "Dad, I get to go to New York City for interviews."

My dad responded, "Ben will like that."

I said, "Yeah, Dad, the schedule of interviews is insane, but hopefully I will get some free time. Can I call you tomorrow? I have to be at the restaurant in, like, twenty minutes and I still need to get dressed."

"Yes, Audrey. Good luck and remember your mother and I love you."

My parents were being abnormally kind to me. It was weird, but it felt good. I said, "Thanks, Dad."

I got dressed and headed out the door. When I got out of the cab in front of Chicago Cut Steakhouse, there was a tall man standing out front who said, "Audrey."

I looked around a little and asked, "Are you talking to me?"

He said, "Yes, I'm Phil, your lawyer."

I said with a sense of relief, "Oh. Hi, Phil."

Phil said, "Pleasure to meet you."

I asked, "Are you ready for this? 'Cause I'm freaking the fuck out because I have no idea what to expect."

"I've made my calls and they want the rights to your book bad because now there's interest from another production company. I know what you deserve so just drink your wine, enjoy your food and let me do the talking."

"I like that idea, Phil."

Phil laughed when he said, "That's why you are paying me the big bucks."

I asked, "How much am I paying you, Phil?"

"Until you sign a movie deal, nothing. Your father and I agreed on ten percent and I'll be by your side for the entire ride."

"Works for me."

"Yes, but I am the last person you will be trusting from here on. No signing anything, no verbal agreements, nothing until it has been run by me. Capisce? Your father told me that you have no idea what is about to come at you and you are very trusting. I've been doing this for three decades and I am telling you that you can't trust anyone. Let me be the bad guy if you want."

I joked and said, "Okay, Bad Guy Phil."

"Very funny, but I am being serious. I've known your father for many years and if it weren't for him I wouldn't be where I am today. He's a good man."

"1 figured it was rare for a Los Angeles entertainment lawyer to fly to Chicago for a new client. I guess I'm lucky my dad knows people."

"You are in good hands. Now let's go discuss and eat."

We sat down and the producer introduced herself before introducing us to her script writer. I wondered why they had no lawyer with them, but just rolled with the punches. We had a lot of small talk, which was fine by me. I was enjoying listening to all the nonsense because I had a glass of wine in my hand. Phil, well, Phil was not so much into small talk. He was the only man at the table though. He insisted we get down to business so the producer took the lead. Damn, I couldn't believe I'd already forgotten the producer's name. Shit. Why was I so bad at remembering names? The producer, whose name I would try to figure out at some point in the night, said, "So, Audrey, we love your story. I mean, we really love it. It is the most real thing I have ever read when it comes to sex, love and timing in one's life."

I asked, "Really?"

"Absolutely. My question is this, though: why do you want your book made into a movie?"

I hesitated. *Was I supposed to be honest here? What had my agent told this producer woman about me?* I took a sip of my wine before answering, giving my agent and lawyer ample time to jump in if they felt so inclined. I finally said, "I didn't even plan to publish the story."

The producer said, "Excuse me?"

I looked at my agent and she gave me a nod to go ahead and tell the truth about what had happened. I said, "I wrote the story for myself to get over a guy."

The producer asked, "Chase Walker?"

"Yes, Chase Walker. I wrote it hoping it would help me move on, but then I accidentally sent it to my agent. She read it and, well, I think you actually read it before I even knew about the mistake I had made."

"So, why move forward?"

"I hesitated at first. I didn't want to expose Chase's life without his permission. More than that, I didn't want to relive the heartache over and over."

"What changed your mind?"

"Seeing how many people were in love and affected by my story, knowing that I had revealed a side of myself that would connect with people in ways that I may never be able to reveal again, and the fact that Chase said he didn't have time to read the story and I could do whatever I wanted."

"So Chase has nothing to do with all this?"

Lawyer Phil cut in and said, "Chase will not be involved in this process. He has already signed documents releasing his rights to the book."

I had no idea Chase had signed his rights away for the book and it stung a little knowing he didn't care enough to read it. I just said, "Phil knows best."

The producer asked, "Do you want Chase involved, Audrey?"

I looked at Phil and he shook his head back and forth at me. I said, "I'm not sure."

The producer said, "I understand. I just want you to understand that he is going to want to and he is going to try to be a part of the movie. He hasn't signed rights away for the movie deal and I can assure you he will care the moment he hears that this book is more than just a sappy love email sent to him. He will push for a piece of the action."

I asked, "How do you know this?"

"I take it you have zero contact with Chase anymore?"

"Nope, I deleted him on Facebook and my friends won't tell me anything. My friend Nikki did mention the MTV reality show fell through, though."

"Audrey, I don't want to interfere with your relationship with him, or lack of a relationship. All I simply want to say is that he's really trying for a reality show with his new lifestyle and piggybacking off this would give him that final push to get it. Just be ready because he may not play nice."

Phil said, "I will be the mediator if Chase feels the need to piggyback off what Audrey is doing."

The producer said, "Phil, I agree that this is Audrey's story. It tells her experience with Chase through her love and her pain, but Chase is going to see it as her exposing his life and stealing his intellectual property."

Phil said, "I've dealt with hundreds of men like Chase. I am not worried."

The producer said, "Alright, let's move on to what it is we are looking for."

I said, "Yeah, help me understand what involvement I will have."

The producer said, "Minimal. Anna..." *Oh, Anna is the script writer's name. Now, if only I could figure out the damn producer's name...* "...has already started scripting your book. Once she is finished, we will fly you out to L.A. to review it with us a few times. We think it's important to have the author's opinion. After the script is complete, we will cast and start production."

I asked, "Can Mila Kunis play me in the movie?"

The producer said, "I'll consider it."

I asked another question, "So, is this going to be a movie for the theatres or is this going to be a made-for-TV movie?"

The producer said, "I haven't made a made-for-TV movie in almost fifteen years. I go big or I go home. I want this on the big screen."

"So, when does all this start?"

"To be honest, Anna has already started on the script, but officially nothing can happen until the rights are bought. You will have our offer in on Monday morning. Your lawyer Phil and my people can duke it out. I will say this: I am going to do my best to make sure you are financially compensated with the most I can get you because I really want to produce this movie. I want to get deep into it and create a movie that makes people feel as much as I felt while reading your book."

"That makes me feel good because as a writer all I've ever wanted to do is connect with people; whether it be emotionally or sexually."

"Girl, you did both in this story. The way you made the reader feel loved by Chase. You pulled us into all those little things he'd say. Seriously, I was right there with you, falling in love with him, too. Then there was the sex. Damn, girl. Finally, the end, where we realize it was all a façade. You were just a convenience and the moment you became an inconvenience to his ultimate goal, he kicked you to the curb."

I asked, "Wait, what?"

"All the psychology you revealed."

Okay, I was a bit confused. Maybe I was starting to get drunk. I didn't think there was that much psychology behind my book, but I wanted to sound smart so I said, "Oh, yeah, the psychology."

The rest of dinner was a bunch of chit-chat,

but amazing food. Phil and I went into the bar for a drink after my agent, the producer, and Anna the script writer left. Phil said we needed to talk numbers, but I told Phil I hated numbers. I was taking a sip of my wine when Phil said he would accept nothing less than one million dollars for the book rights along with me having 20% ownership in the production of the film. I nearly spat out my wine. I never expected those kinds of numbers. He then went on to say that merchandising was a whole other ballgame. I told Phil I was too drunk for any more numbers so we should do a shot and call it a night. Phil shook his head back and forth at me, but then agreed. He said he'd be calling me tomorrow to discuss numbers. We took our shots down like champs and I guzzled the rest of my wine before Phil walked me out to a cab and sent me home. My drunk ass decided to call my parents and when my dad answered the phone he asked, "How did it go?"

I said, "Dad, I am going to be a bajillionaire."

I could tell I had been placed on speaker phone when my dad said, "A bajillionaire, eh?"

"What can I say; they love me. I'm going to be famous and Mila Kunis is going to play me in the movie."

My mom cut in and said, "Audrey, are you drunk?"

I said, "Noooooooooooooo, Mom, I'm not drunk, but I am a liar."

My mom said, "Oh, smooth, you sound like your grandmother with that one."

My dad said, "It sounds like you had a good time. Phil will take care of the logistics, so don't worry."

My mom said, "Do you think Audrey ever worries about that stuff?"

I said, "Hey now, I might be drunk, but I can still comprehend what you are saying."

My dad said, "You should be proud of yourself, so go out and celebrate. Call us tomorrow when your hangover is gone."

"Okay, Dad. Goodnight. I love you guys."

I woke up the next morning to a pounding at my door and a pounding in my head. I rolled out of bed still dressed in my clothes from the night before. Crap, what the fuck happened? The last thing I remember was calling my parents and telling them I was going to be a bajillionaire. The pounding at the door continued so I made my way there and opened it up. There was a young man standing on the other side with a box. He asked, "Are you Audrey Buchanan?"

I said, "Yes."

He said, "These are for you and here's a note. Have a nice day."

I closed the door and walked over to my kitchen table. I set down the box of Glazed and Infused donuts, but opened it up and took one out to eat while I read the note. With a mouth full of an old-fashioned donut I read the note that said, "You are going to make an amazing bajillionaire."

The note didn't say who it was from. *Did my parents really just send me a box of donuts?* I walked over and found my phone on the couch next to a glass of wine. I took a look at my recent calls and saw that I was on the phone with Ben for a half-hour after I had talked to my parents. Fuck, I had talked to him while I was blacked out. Lord knows what kind of shit I said. Just to be sure it was Ben who'd sent the donuts, I sent him a text that said, "Thanks for the donuts" with the donut emoticon and a heart after it.

A few minutes later Ben responded, "I heard donuts are good for hangovers." *Fuck, I didn't even want to know what I said.* Another text came in that said, "Great conversation last night. I'm looking forward to next weekend."

Shitballs, I'd said too much. Half of me wanted to call him and find out what I'd said, but the other half of me knew that it was better to pretend it had never happened. I took down two more donuts then finally took my clothes off from the night before and washed my face. Once I felt all clean and full, I crawled back into bed and put on the movie *An Affair to Remember* on my iPad. It was one of those movies that seemed to get better each time I watched it.

The week was pretty annoying. Steven had me busy every single day with photo shoots, practice interviews, wardrobe, a makeover, and other various events. Luckily, I had Friday afternoon open so I could pick Ben up from the airport. I'd planned to drive to pick him up, but he had gone all out when I visited him so I hopped on my phone and got an Uber SUV limo. When I'd been drunk I'd believed I'd be a bajillionaire, so I might as well start acting like one. The Uber picked me up and drove me to the airport. I had him stop at a liquor store on the way for some champagne. I wanted to be fancy. When the limo pulled up to O'Hare Airport I saw Ben walking out of the door. I pointed him out to the driver and when we pulled up near him, I hopped out of the limo and yelled, "Ben!"

Ben looked over at me and smiled. Seeing his smile made me excited to see him so I ran over to him and gave him a big welcoming hug. Ben said, "What a great way to be welcomed to Chicago!"

We got into the limo and headed to my apartment. I told Ben I wanted to stay in that night to rest up. It had been an annoyingly busy week and the next day was going to be a late one. He said he was just happy to be here spending time with me. We ordered a Lou Malnati's pizza, one of the best deep dish pizzas in Chicago, and I poured us each a glass of wine. We cuddled up on the couch and talked about the book launch event and what each of us would be doing for Thanksgiving that next week. As Ben was telling me how he was flying to California to visit his family for the holiday weekend, there was a loud knock on my door. I jumped up with excitement and said, "The pizza is here! Damn, that was fast!"

I sort of danced as I walked to the door and when I opened it, I had a smile on my face. That smile quickly went away and my stomach dropped. Chase was standing on the other side of the door. I was speechless. I didn't know why he was at my door and his mere presence made me feel so ill inside that I couldn't even form words in my mouth. I just looked at Chase until I saw him raise his left hand and point his finger at me as he said, "Fuck you, Audrey! Fuck you for taking my life and exposing it to the world." I was still speechless. I didn't know how to respond. I stood there quietly as Chase went on, "How the fuck could you do that? I mean, I've dated some crazy bitches, but a girl who writes a book about me after we break up takes the cake."

Ben came to the door and cut in. He said, "Audrey, are you okay?"

I gave Ben a look like I wasn't okay, but words were still not forming in my mouth. Ben looked at Chase and said, "Hey, man, I think you should go."

Chase asked, "Who the fuck are you? Are you her next victim that she uses to get a good story?"

Ben said, "I really think it's time you leave," and he shut the door in Chase's face.

Chase yelled through the door, "Fuck you both!"

I looked at Ben and said, "I'm sorry. That's Chase."

Ben smiled at me and said, "I figured. Don't worry about him," as he pulled me in to hug me before kissing me on my forehead. My stomach was in knots, but Ben made me feel comfortable. For me, a kiss on the forehead was like a kiss on a child's booboo. Ben calmed me down and then suggested I call my PR agent Steven and let him know what had happened. He was worried that Chase might try to ruin my book launch party the next night. I did as Ben suggested and called Steven to tell him about what had happened. Steven told me not to worry and that he would take care of it. I felt a sense of relief when Steven told me not to worry.

It was still pretty early It, but Ben and I decided to cuddle up in bed. I felt incredibly safe around him. We lay with our heads on the pillows chatting for quite a bit before I pulled out my iPad and asked what movie he wanted to watch. When I swiped my iPad to turn it on, the credits screen for *An Affair to Remember* showed up. Ben asked what movie the credits were from. I told him and he said he had never seen that movie, but had heard about it. He asked if we could watch it.

I asked, "Really?"

Ben said, "Yeah, why? Is it not a movie guys would like?"

I said, "It's a love story."

Ben laughed and said, "Guys like love stories, too."

"Good, let's watch it! It is one of my all-time favorite movies!"

Ben asked, "Is it that good?"

I said with excitement, "Absolutely!"

Ben and I cuddled up watching *An Affair to Remember*. I fell asleep halfway into the movie, but woke up in the middle of the night with cramping in my stomach. Not period cramps, but some serious gas cramps. I slowly moved out of the spooning position Ben and I were in because my ass was backed up on him and I was scared I was going to fart on his balls. When I'd got out of the spoon, I lay there for a few moments thinking about my stomach and the gas pains moving through it. When I'd fallen asleep and finally relaxed, that knot Chase put my stomach in must've come undone. I could feel the gas pains moving faster through the many feet of bowels so I thought it might be wise to sneak out of the bedroom to allow the release of whatever it was that was working its way through my bowels with vengeance. As I moved to sit up though, a huge fart came out of my ass that sounded like a bomb and literally rocked the bed. Ben sat up and asked, "What was that noise? My face was full of embarrassment and I didn't respond. Ben continued by asking, "Did you fart?

I responded, "No, I didn't fart," but then I started laughing knowing I was lying. There was no way he'd believe me that I didn't fart with the retched smell that was surrounding us.

Ben said, "That is the worst fart I have ever smelled in my life."

I kept laughing and said, "It was pretty epic considering it woke you up and you can sleep through almost anything.

Ben said, "I can't believe something like that came out of a pretty little thing like you."

I said, "My stomach was in a knot after Chase showed up. My farts aren't usually that bad."

Ben said, "Let's pretend it never happened. I much prefer to go back to thinking girls don't fart." "Ben, if you are going to be hanging out with me it is going to be hard to pretend that girls don't fart. I am not much of a lady."

Ben kissed me on the forehead and then pulled me close to spoon me as he said, "Well, let me pretend for a little while."

The next morning I woke up to Ben kissing my forehead before he said, "Wake up, my little farting princess. Today is your big day!"

I laughed and asked, "What time is it?"

Ben said, "Almost 10, so we need to get moving."

I said, "Nuh-uh, I don't have to go get my hair and make-up done until 4"

Ben said, "I have a little surprise for you. We are going to a spa for a couple's massage."

My eyes widened before I asked, "Are we really?"

"Yes, now get up; we have to get going."

I said, "Yes, sir!"

We went to our spa day at The Peninsula Hotel and then came home to relax for a little bit before I had to go to get my hair and make-up done for my book launch. While I was getting pretty, everyone kept texting me asking me questions about the event. My mom didn't know what to wear. Nikki wanted to see if she could bring a different guy from the one she'd put on her RSVP. Bree asked if it was okay if she was a little late. I answered all the questions coming in via text and once my phone was quiet I hopped on my Twitter to tweet about my excitement for the event that night. I looked at my mentions before composing the tweet and there was one from a girl named Vivian who I didn't recognize. The tweet said, "@AudreyBWrites you may have written a book about him, but he's fucking me now."

I thought: *What the hell?* Who was this girl? I took a look at her profile and saw she was some aspiring model. I tried to forget about it, but something like that isn't easy to forget. I closed down my Twitter and looked up with a sad look on my face. Andrea, the girl doing my hair, asked, "Is everything okay?"

Even though I wasn't feeling fine, I said, "Yeah, everything is fine."

She said, "Good, I'm almost finished here and then Gia will get started on your make-up."

When I got home Ben was waiting for me. He said, "Audrey, you look so beautiful!" when I walked into my apartment.

I smiled and said, "Thank you."

Ben asked, "What's wrong?"

"Oh, nothing."

Ben said, "Something isn't right. Are you sure you don't want to talk about it?"

I said, "Well, I guess I can tell you." I grabbed my phone and opened my Twitter app. I clicked on the mentions and said, "Come here and look at this."

Ben came in close and looked. He asked, "What am I looking for?"

I said, "Read the first tweet in my mentions."

Ben asked, "The one from Nikki that says good luck tonight?"

I looked at my phone as I said, "No, not that one. This one..." I looked further down and noticed the tweet was gone. I continued by saying, "That's odd. There was a tweet from a girl that said, 'You may have written a book about him, but he's fucking me now.'"

Ben said, "Who was the girl?"

I said, "I don't know, her profile said she was a model or something."

I searched for the girl's name, but the tweet wasn't on her profile. *Was I losing my mind?* Ben said, "Maybe she deleted it?"

I said, "Maybe. Oh well, let's forget about it. We need to get ready for the party!"

We got ready and enjoyed a small glass of wine before heading over to Hotel 71 for my book launch event. I'd been told to arrive forty-five minutes after the start time of the event to look cool or some shit. We pulled up in the black town car and Steven was outside waiting for my arrival. I got out of the car first and he said, "Oh, Audrey, you look stunning."

I smiled and said, "Thank you."

Steven said, "Okay, when you get inside smile for the cameras, strike a pose, shake some hands, and kiss some babies."

I laughed and said, "Okay," as I grabbed Ben's hand to walk with me.

Steven said, "Sorry, date, you can't walk in with Audrey. Just follow shortly behind her."

I said, "Wait, why can't he walk with me?"

My book agent said, "Audrey, didn't I say never to question Steven?"

Where the hell did she come from? I said, "Hi."

My agent said, "You look beautiful, dear, now go walk; proud of yourself and your story."

I looked at Ben and said, "I'm sorry."

He smiled back and said, "Don't worry, I can take care of myself, but if you need anything, just let me know."

I blew Ben a kiss and walked into the area where my event was. The cameras started flashing and I thought: *Holy shit, it's like the damn paparazzi!* I didn't understand any of this. How did so many people get interested in my book in such a short period of time? What kind of magic was Steven playing? I just went with it and smiled away. I should've had a much larger glass of wine before this event though. I didn't have time to scratch the itch on my ass, let alone get a drink to calm my nerves. After an hour, things finally slowed down a bit and I was able to say hello to my parents. Ben had introduced himself to my parents and my mother thought he was a doll. My dad reminded me how proud he was of me and then said, "Don't worry about us. Get back out there and be a celebrity, kiddo!" I smiled at my father and then took the glass of wine out of his hand and walked away. As I was walking away he said, "Enjoy my wine."

Enjoy his wine I did and I chugged it all down before looking for Nikki and Bree. I got stopped by several people before I found Nikki and Bree though. Once I did, I felt relaxed. It felt good to be surrounded by friends for a few minutes. As we were standing and talking, I waved at Ben to come join our conversation. As he was walking toward us, Bree leaned in and said, "My God, that boy Ben is in love with you."

I said, "He's not in love. We are just getting to know one another."

Nikki cut in and said, "Dude, he's in love.

Like, head over heels. Probably would marry your ass tomorrow if he could."

I said, "Stop, you guys."

When Ben walked up, I smiled at him and asked if he was having fun. He said, "I've met a lot of interesting people here tonight and I've talked you up to the media quite a bit."

Nikki asked with a snickering laugh, "Did you tell them Audrey is your girlfriend?"

I felt my face get flushed and I saw Ben's get flushed too, but he calmly said, "No, Nikki, I referred to Audrey as a friend."

Nikki said, "Lame. You should give these media people some gossip."

I said, "I'm sure they have plenty to run on. I haven't told you about last night yet."

Nikki asked, "What happened last night?"

As I went to answer Nikki to tell her about Chase showing up at my door, I heard Steven yell, "Audrey, Audrey, come here! We need you."

I said, "Ben, can you tell Nikki and Bree what happened last night?"

Ben said, "Yeah, go do your thing, Miss Celebrity," as he lightly patted my ass.

I smiled at Ben and walked toward Steven. He introduced me to a guy named Zach, who was the host of a local TV show. I remembered seeing a couple of episodes of his talk show, but he was much hotter in person. After Steven introduced us he said, "You are going to be on Zach's talk show Wednesday."

I asked, "I am?"

Zach let out a little laugh. Steven said, "Yes, you are, darling. Check your calendar."

Steven walked away and I said to Zach,

"Sorry, I am not very good at keeping track of stuff like that."

Zach said, "I understand."

Zach and I talked for a little while and I could see why so many women were smitten with this guy. He was hot and chill. Plus, he was on TV. I'm sure he had women chasing him all around town. When I spotted Wayne, I excused myself to go and say hello. Wayne asked to get on the event list because he had a date he wanted to impress. His date looked like a bottle service girl and didn't seem like his type at all. The entire time I was talking with them I was wondering if this girl had had a chance to see the itty bitty penis and blonde, hairy shag carpet in his pants yet? How could such a nice guy have such a small dick? You'd think God would give the nice guys big dicks instead of the assholes.

I talked to Wayne and his date, Ariana, for a few minutes before Steven stole me away to introduce me to more people. I can't recall all the other people I met, but according to Steven they were super important people. They all seemed nice, but my feet were starting to hurt and I couldn't wait to get home. Luckily, the room started to clear out and I was able to take down a few glasses of wine. Once the room was almost empty, Ben and I said our goodbyes and headed home.

When Ben and I got home, I took my dress off the moment I walked in the door. Ben told me I was a tease for getting naked in front of him. I was high off my pseudo-celebrity appearance and I was really starting to like Ben so I walked up to him and kissed him. He kissed me back, but I could feel his hesitation. I wrapped my legs around him and jumped up. He held me and walked us into my bedroom. We continued kissing as he slowly set me down on the bed. Once I was on the bed Ben asked, "Are you sure you are ready?"

I responded, "I'm sure," as I worked to take his belt off.

He asked, "Are you sure, sure?"

I said, "Yes; don't ruin the moment - kiss me!"

Ben kissed me with passion and I felt the excitement building in my body. Butterflies were fluttering in my stomach. I could feel it; I was ready. As Ben kissed me, he held my face lightly with his left hand and gently ran the fingers on his right hand up and down my body. I could feel my pussy getting wet as his fingers moved down the side of my body and onto my thigh. I wanted his cock inside of me immediately. I was feeling so turned on, but his lips moved off mine and down my neck. As he continued down my body, he stopped to caress my breasts and lick my nipples. I felt them get hard from being turned on and the cold air from the fan breezing past them while they were wet. Ben continued moving his lips down past my stomach until they gently hit my pussy. I could feel the cum exiting my pussy. He moved his tongue up and down my labia, gently teasing my clit. I wanted him to ravish my clit.

He was so gentle with my pussy and it felt good, but I was ready to get fucked. I wanted to feel him inside me so I sat up and pushed him over onto his back. I kissed him passionately and considered putting his cock in my mouth, but I wanted his cock inside of my pussy so badly that I decided to be selfish and I sat down on his cock slowly. The initial penetration of his cock felt so good. I felt my pussy grab it tightly with enthusiasm. I moved my hips up and down on his cock, moaning with each thrust. When I looked down, I could see my cum covering his cock. It turned me on even more.

I rode his cock for several minutes before I couldn't take it anymore. I wanted him to take control of my body, of my mind, to fuck me hard, and to make me orgasm. I got off Ben's cock and got on all fours as I told him to fuck me from behind. Ben got behind me, but then wrapped his arms around me, grasping my boobs with his hands. He pulled me up and said, "Not tonight, darling. I want to see you while I feel you."

Ben turned me around and pushed me down so I was lying on my back. He pushed his cock inside me with force and it felt euphoric. He moved in and out of me, going faster with each thrust. It felt good, almost too good because I was ready to orgasm. I wanted to hold on longer and I tried, but my body became too tense and my pussy began to pulsate in orgasm. As I embraced my pussy pulsating around his cock, I felt his cock also pulsate and release in orgasm. A few moments later, Ben crashed down on the bed next to me then leaned over and kissed me on the forehead. My whole body was fluttering with orgasm, but his kiss on my forehead sent even more butterflies through my body. After a few minutes of catching our breaths and cooling off, Ben pulled me in to hold me tight. In a matter of moments I fell asleep in his arms.

When I woke up in the morning, Ben wasn't holding me tight. He wasn't even in the bed, but I heard the shower running and him singing so I rolled my naked body out of bed and walked into the bathroom. As I walked into the bathroom, I laughed when I realized what song Ben was singing. He was singing One Direction's *What Makes You Beautiful*. I giggled a little when I pulled my toothbrush and toothpaste out of the cabinet as he sang, "Everyone else in the room can see it. Everyone else, but you." Then he burst open the curtains and continued singing buck naked into the shampoo bottle, "Baby, you light up my world like nobody else. The way you flip your hair gets me overwhelmed! But when you smile at the ground it ain't hard to tell. You don't know oh oh... You don't know you're beautiful."

I couldn't help but giggle more as he sang on. I spat out the toothpaste in my mouth and hopped into the shower with Ben. I kissed him, and while I was kissing him he said, "You are beautiful, Audrey."

I giggled like a little schoolgirl and kept kissing him until I felt his cock poking my stomach. Once I felt it was hard enough I turned around, placing my hands on the shower wall. I slightly bent over and Ben slowly penetrated my pussy until his cock was fully immersed inside me. He moved in and out of me, slowly at first, while holding my hips, but he quickly sped up. I moaned in pleasure and then I heard him moan. He moved his left arm off my hip and grabbed my left boob from behind. As he squeezed my boob, I could feel my pussy squeezing his cock tighter and tighter.

I was enjoying each thrust thoroughly, but suddenly Ben pulled out and came on my ass. As he was coming he said, "I'm so sorry."

I was disappointed, but I didn't let him know. I just turned around, smiled and then kissed him. A man prematurely ejaculating was disappointing, but at the same time it was a huge compliment. I washed the cum off my ass, shampooed my hair, and washed my face before we got out of the shower. Once out of the shower we dried off and got dressed. Ben had to be at the airport in forty-five minutes so he packed his stuff up and we headed out of the door.

When we walked up to my car Ben asked, "Is this your car?"

I answered, "Yes."

He asked, "Does it drive?"

I laughed a little inside because my vintage BMW didn't look like it could move, but I said, "Yes, it's a great car."

Ben said, "You make plenty of money with your books so why do you drive such an old car?"

I said, "I don't know. I don't drive very often, but I have been thinking about buying a new car."

"For safety reasons, I think you should."

I said, "Shut up, it's perfectly safe."

Ben said, "Whatever you say, my dear."

The first few days of my week were very busy. I was on everything from the radio station KISS FM to the TV talk show *Windy City Live*. It was fun, but exhausting at the same time. Every day I had a couple of interviews and I was already over it. On Wednesday night, the night before Thanksgiving, I considered driving out to my parents', but decided to stay home and get some writing done. While I was writing an article for the RedEye newspaper, I heard a knock on my door. I wasn't sure who would be knocking on my door on a Wednesday night because I hadn't ordered pizza or any food. When I walked up to the door I wished I had one of those peepholes to see who was knocking before I opened it. I didn't have a peephole so I slowly opened my door and saw Chase standing on the other side. I was speechless so I just stood there looking at him, waiting for him to yell at me. Chase looked at me and said, "Your book is beautiful and it is the best gift anyone has ever given me."

I wasn't sure how to respond so I just stood on the other side of the door looking at him. Chase took a step toward me and said, "Audrey, I miss you."

I took a step back, away from Chase, and said, "Chase, don't say that."

Chase took another step closer to me and shut the door behind him before he said, "Audrey, I really did love your book. It was a great depiction of our relationship."

I took another step back and asked, "Why are you here, Chase?"

Chase said, "I wanted to see you."

I asked, "Why?"

Chase responded, "I don't know. I read your book and something inside me said I needed to see you."

I said, "I don't think you should be here, Chase."

Chase asked, "Why not?"

I said, "I don't know. I just don't think I should be around you."

Chase said, "Audrey, I know you are still in love with me. You wrote an entire book on how good of a lover I am. It's okay. I am that great, so I wouldn't expect anything less from a past lover."

I said, "Chase, I think you should leave."

Chase said, "No, I know and you know; you don't want me to leave right now. I've read your book and I know I am the best lover you have ever had or will have, so let me get close to you."

"Chase, no. I think you should leave."

Chase walked closer to me and I took another step back, but my step back wasn't far enough. Chase gently grabbed the back of my neck and pulled me in for a kiss. I kissed him back. I couldn't help it. I missed him and his touch, even though I didn't want to. Chase kissed me hard and passionately and I loved the way it felt. When he picked my body up and carried me into the bedroom I didn't fight it because I was so turned on. I could feel the cum exiting my pussy and gathering on my panties.

Chase set me down on the bed before he pulled off my sweatpants and panties. I felt a little embarrassed because my pussy was a little scruffy. I hadn't shaved in a few days because I wasn't expecting to get laid again for a while. After he pulled my pants off, he went down and gently began licking my pussy. I felt it getting more wet with each lick. I was so turned on, but he said, "I love licking your pussy, but I want to be inside you. I can't hold out any longer."

While Chase undressed in front of me, I pulled my shirt off over my head. Once he was naked, he got on top of me and pushed his cock inside my pussy. The initial penetration sent shivers through my body. I closed my eyes, enjoying each thrust he made into my pussy. As my eyes were closed though, I remembered the agony I went through when Chase left me. I thought to myself: *What the hell am I doing?* I opened my eyes and told Chase to get off me. He asked, "Why? Aren't you enjoying this?"

I said, "No, I am not."

Chase said, "Your pussy is so wet. I think you are."

With aggression I said, "No, Chase. I can't do this."

Chase asked, "Why not?"

"This isn't right. I can't go through this again. You need to leave."

"Hold on now, Audrey. Let's talk about

this."

I asked, "What is there to talk about?"

Chase said, "Why I am here."

"Why are you here? Do you want to get back together?"

"Audrey, I care about you deeply and I miss sex with you."

I asked Chase again, "Are you here to get back together?"

Chase said, "No, but I want to connect with you again."

"What do you mean, 'connect with me?'"

I got off the bed and began putting my clothes on when Chase said, "I've got a lot going on and, well, you and I were just getting too serious for me at this time in my life. I think we should stay connected."

I asked, "Stay connected for what?"

"I've entered a spiritual phase in my life and I want to try some things before I settle down with someone. I've learned something about myself and it has led me to a place where I am ready to try a new sort of relationship. I'd love it if you were open to this kind of relationship with me."

I asked, "What the fuck are you talking about, Chase?"

Chase said, "I've been meditating a lot and I've learned that I am an Indigo Child."

I asked, "You're blue?"

With seriousness Chase said, "No, I am at a higher spiritual level than most and I can connect with ethereal beings."

I asked, "Are you on drugs? What the hell are you talking about?"

"Audrey, don't judge me. Embrace this. I

am a higher power and I can do things most can't. I can cleanse people, heal, rid people of jealousy, and so much more."

I walked out of the bedroom and said, "I need a fucking drink."

Chase followed me into the kitchen as I was pouring myself a hefty glass of wine. He said, "Audrey, haven't you felt the love I've been sending you since we broke up?"

I chugged down the entire glass of wine before I responded. While I was pouring myself another glass of wine I said, "Fuck no, Chase. You fucking left me and then you showed up here yelling at me for writing about my experience dating you."

"I am very sorry about that. I lost my spiritual control that night. I was wrong and after I finally read your story due to the hype, I realized it was beautiful. It not only made me realize how in love with me you are, but it also made me realize that you will wait for me."

With attitude I said, "Wait for you? What?"

"Now that I know my powers, I need to have one last experience that I've always wanted to have. With finding these powers within myself, I now know I am ready to take it on."

"Powers? Do you think you're a *Teenage Mutant Ninja Turtle* or something?"

"You've always loved those *Teenage Mutant Ninja Turtles*, but no I am not some made-up character. I am real and I have the ability to change the way people love for the better."

I filled my glass of wine all the way to the top and then walked over to the couch. I asked,

"How can you change the way people love, Chase?"

"I can prove that people can have relationships that eradicate jealousy."

"Excuse me?"

"I am involved in a relationship right now." My stomach dropped. This asshole broke up with me because he said he needed to be single and he was already in a relationship?

"Seriously, Chase, you are in a fucking relationship? You said you had to leave me to be single!"

"It's not what you think; I'm in a group relationship."

I asked, "A what?"

"I am in a group relationship with two women. I am dating them both and they are dating each other. We may even add a fourth."

"What the fuck?"

"It's sharing love within a group where there is no jealousy. We love each other freely. We give each other permissions and share sexual experiences."

I was so confused. What the hell was he talking about? I asked, "Permissions?"

"Yes, we come as one, but allow permissions to share our love with other people. So if one of us wants to venture out of the group and sleep with another person, we give permissions to allow them to share their love."

I said, "What the fuck?"

Chase tilted his head at me like he was going to reprimand me when he said, "Don't judge, Audrey. I know if you had an open mind then you'd understand what I am saying."

I asked, "Why did you never mention this when we were dating?"

"I did, remember? I wasn't ready yet either, but I was always suggesting we have a threesome to start working us toward this."

"I just thought you wanted a sexual experience. I had no idea you wanted me to date girls."

"I knew you'd struggle with it, but hoped with time you would warm up to it and understand the beauty in it."

"Damn straight, I'd struggle with it. Why would I want to share my man?"

Chase asked, "Audrey, can I do a meditation with you?"

I asked with a snarky tone, "What, are you going to try to brainwash me?"

"No, I want to cleanse your mind and body so you can understand me better."

I sat staring at Chase like he was nuts and I didn't answer him. His phone had been ringing off the hook for several minutes so I asked, "Are you going to answer your phone, or what?"

"It's nothing urgent. Let me do this meditation. I want you to feel the energy come out of me so we can connect."

I chugged the rest of my wine and said, "Fine."

Chase went into my bedroom and lit some candles while I refilled my glass of wine. When I walked into the room, he had my iPad playing some relaxing music. He told me to lie down on the bed and take deep breaths. I took a few sips of my wine before I did what he asked. When I sat down I took some deep breaths and closed my eyes. The music was relaxing and I had a nice warm buzz tingling through my body from the wine. I lay there face up, taking breaths, when I felt Chase moving his hands over my body. I waited for something magical to happen. Maybe Jesus would appear or my grandpa would tell me some news from the dead. I wasn't sure what to expect. I sat there and suddenly Chase began making moaning noises. Soon those moaning noises turned into sounds from his mouth imitating waves crashing in the ocean. I wanted to burst out laughing, but he was being so serious.

I tried to play along for several minutes, but I wanted to laugh so badly. I fought and fought the laughter until I couldn't take it anymore and I started silently laughing; the kind of laughter that makes no sound, but makes your body shake. Holding in such a big laughter was hard and my eyes started watering. I was dying there with Chase doing his voodoo over me and all I could think was: *What the hell happened to Chase?* I mean, finding yourself is great, but he'd gone from a straight-edged, logical man to an Indigo Child in a matter of weeks. Everything I had learned about him in the past hour made me feel completely turned off by him. This was good. Maybe all this voodoo stuff was God's way of helping me move on. Oh, that God worked in tricky ways.

When Chase finished his voodoo meditations with me, he got off the bed and walked out of the bedroom. I wondered where the hell he'd gone. While he was gone, I grabbed my phone off the nightstand to see if anyone had called. When I looked at it, there were a bunch of text messages from a Vivian that said things like, "Where the fuck are you?" "Call me now!" and "Are you with her?" I realized I had picked up the wrong phone. Whoever this Vivian girl was must not have learned the ridding of jealousy thing yet. I put his phone down and looked around the room for my phone, but Chase walked back in the bedroom and handed me a glass of water. He said, "It's good to stay hydrated after a meditation like that." I thought to myself that rehydrating after laughter like that was probably a good thing. Chase continued, "I could feel your body shaking and the tears let me know that you were really connecting with me. The energy between us was so high."

Our energy was so high? He really had no idea I had been silently laughing. Well, the good thing was that this little escapade was exactly what I needed to move on from Chase. I needed a little push in the right direction and he handed it to me on a silver platter. I was glad he was happy, but the world in which he lived was something that wasn't for me. I didn't want group relationships and although I was spiritual, I wasn't at a level at which I'd believe something like, "Jesus told me I am an Indigo Child."

Chase didn't stay much longer. His phone was ringing non-stop and he seemed agitated. I was relieved when he left. I felt so much anxiety when he showed up at my door, but the series of events made me think that him breaking up with me was okay. He really was moving into a new direction in his life, a direction that was interesting, but beyond what

I knew or believed.

Thursday morning, Thanksgiving, I woke up really early to get out to my parents' house in time to see Santa arrive on the *Macy's Thanksgiving Day Parade*. It was a tradition. We'd watch Santa arrive and then eat a champagne brunch. It was the perfect combination of some of the things I loved most: the Christmas season and alcohol. I bundled up and headed out of the door to my car, but as I was approaching my car, I noticed it had been vandalized. Once I got close, I saw the tires were flat, the word "whore" was keyed on my hood and there were dents on the side like someone had kicked it. I didn't understand why someone would do something like that. I had received a few blocked calls the night before when Chase was over, but I thought nothing of it because telemarketers were always annoying me.

I called my father to tell him what had happened and he told me to take some photos and call the police right away. He said he was putting his coat on and heading downtown to come and get me. I took a few photos and called the police while I walked back into my apartment. It was too fucking cold to stand outside and wait for them. I stopped for a donut at the Dunkin Donuts across the street before heading up to my apartment. I figured it would be a while. I sat looking out of the back window of my apartment from where I could see my car in the distance. I watched as the snow flurries fell and wondered why this had happened. I guessed maybe it was a sign that I should finally buy myself a new car. I did have plenty of money now so I could buy myself something ridiculously fancy like I had planned.

I saw a Chicago police SUV rolling down the street so I walked downstairs really fast to catch them. The police officer had me fill out a report and while I was filling it out, my father pulled up. He got out of the car and gave me a big hug while he asked, "Are you okay?"

I said, "Yeah, Dad, I'm fine, but my poor car isn't."

My dad squeezed me tight when he said, "I'm glad you are okay. A car can be fixed, but I don't know what your mother and I would do if something happened to you."

"Dad, it's probably just some crazy religious person who doesn't like that I write about sex."

My dad and I talked to the policeman and then had a tow truck come to take away my car. We decided to worry about it after Thanksgiving. My dad drove me out to our family's lake house. My mom gave me a big hug when I arrived. I assured her I was fine. She surprised us by showing my dad and me that she had figured out how to DVR the *Macy's Thanksgiving Day Parade* so we wouldn't miss Santa's arrival. It made me smile.

I spent the next few days with my family. It was nice to see my grandma, aunts, uncles, and cousins. They were all enthralled by my new local celebrity status. On Sunday, my father drove me back to the city in the morning so I could pack. Luckily, I didn't have to make any decisions on what to wear because the clothing boutique Akira had given me outfits to wear at each interview.

I had an afternoon flight I had to catch to Los Angeles for some radio interviews that week. Steven picked me up in a town car and we headed to the airport. For the entire car ride there, he seemed to be barking orders at me. At the gate and until it was okay to turn on electronic devices, we went over interview questions. Steven didn't trust that I'd say the right things and neither did I. I have an awkward tendency to speak before I think.

Once the flight attendant gave us the okay to turn on electronic devices, I went to work on writing blog posts. I had to figure out how to write a sexy and sassy blog about my personal life and experiences. The first post I decided to write was about firsts, kicking it off with the story of how I lost my virginity. Not one of my proudest moments, but as Steven sat next to me on the plane watching the words I was writing, he said that what I was saying was something every person could relate to.

I pumped that post out pretty fast. The second post, well, since I had just had an unsuccessful sexual encounter with my ex, Chase, I figured writing about hooking up with an ex-boyfriend might be a good post. Steven continued watching me and again thought it was marvelous. It was weird having someone sit next to me and watch me as I wrote.

As I sipped on the cheap wine the flight

attendant brought me, I tried to think of other blog post ideas. From masturbation to farting at your boyfriend's house, I churned up a dozen ideas. It was nearing landing time though, so I closed down my computer and finished off the second glass of cheap-ass wine I was drinking. I figured I'd have plenty of time in hotel rooms alone over the next few weeks to write up posts about all the ideas I had just come up with.

We landed and took a car to our hotel. I asked Steven if he wanted to grab dinner, but he said he had some friends in Los Angeles that he was going to go and visit. He didn't invite me along. I decided to eat at the hotel bar alone. When I was finished eating, I decided to order one last glass of wine before heading upstairs to call it a night. While I was drinking my wine and people-watching, a very attractive girl sat down next to me. She asked, "Are you here for the seminar?"

I responded, "No, I have some interviews tomorrow."

She asked, "Interviews for what?"

I said, "For my book that was just released."

She asked yet another question, which is standard when two people have just met. "What's the name of your book?"

I said, "*Dating Chase Walker*."

Sounding a little taken aback, she said, "Shut the fuck up! That's your book?"

I said, "Yes."

She said, "I heard about that book."

I asked, "Do you have a copy?"

"Not yet."

"I can run upstairs and get you one. I have a bunch in my hotel room if you want one."

She asked, "Really? Can you sign it, too?"

I said, "Yeah."

She said, "I'm Olivia by the way."

I responded, "I'm Audrey."

Olivia ordered a drink and we chatted for a couple of hours. She was really cool. Three glasses of wine after what I had thought would be my last glass of wine for the night, I realized I had to be up in five hours for a radio interview. I told Olivia I should probably call it a night. She asked if she could come up with me to get a copy of my book. I had forgotten I had offered her a copy. She ordered us each one more glass of wine to go before we left the bar. When I stood up from the bar, I realized I did not need another glass of wine because I was lucky to be able to stand.

As Olivia looked around my room, she said how much bigger mine was than hers. I took out a copy of *Dating Chase Walker* to sign and give her. When I went to hand it to Olivia, she put her hand on the back of my neck and pulled me close to her. She kissed me hard and passionately and even though I was completely taken aback by her kiss, I found her extremely attractive and kissed her back. I was instantly turned on and felt my pussy fluttering with excitement. Olivia pulled my shirt off over my head and unhooked my bra. Once my bare breasts were out, she moved her lips down to lick my nipples.

As I felt my nipples get harder, I also felt the cum begin to exit my pussy. Normally, I was turned on by the strength and manly scent of a big burly man, but at that moment I was turned on by the tenderness and connection of being with a woman. It created such a different feeling inside me and, since being with a woman was a new experience, it made it exciting. Olivia moved down from licking my nipples to tenderly caressing my stomach with her hands and mouth. I felt her pull my pants down and in that moment I realized that I hadn't showered since the night before and I had been traveling all day so my pussy most likely was repping some rankness. I led her back up and kissed her. After kissing me she asked, "Why don't you want me to go down on you?"

I said, "It's been a while since I showered and I've been traveling all day."

She said, "I'm sure it's fine. Let me taste your pussy."

I said, "I'm going to be worried about the stench the whole time so I won't enjoy it."

Olivia smiled at me and said, "Let's take a quick shower," as she pulled her shirt off over her head and began walking toward the bathroom.

I followed Olivia to the bathroom and watched her as she finished undressing. Her body was amazing and I was confused that I was turned on by a woman. Once the water was warm, Olivia got into the shower and I followed. Under the spout of water, she kissed me. While she was kissing me, she filled her hand up with the hotel body wash and then slowly caressed it between my legs. Feeling the bubbles form over my pussy was such a turn on. As I took in the feeling of her hand slowly moving over my clit, I used my hand to caress her breasts. Her small, real breasts felt nothing like my hard, perky, fake breasts. Moving my hand down from her breast, I began slowly rubbing my hand over her pussy. I wasn't sure what I was doing and I think she noticed because she gently put her hand on mine and led it up and down. I had never felt another pussy in my life. It was strange, but interesting to me.

Olivia led me out of the shower and turned off the water. I handed her a towel and then took one off the shelf to dry myself off. Once dry, we walked out to the bed and she sat down. She looked at me and told me she wanted me to lick her pussy. *Fuck, I didn't know how to munch a rug.* After she had laid down on her back, I obliged and crawled in between her legs. Dozens of memories of men who had gone down on me ran through my mind and with each memory that came I took ideas on how I could satisfy Olivia's pussy with my tongue. After licking up and down, I took my index finger and slowly inserted it into her pussy. I heard Olivia moan in pleasure. I pushed my middle finger into her pussy with my index finger and she moaned louder. I knew that when a man was inside me, pushing at the top of the entryway of the pussy was the hot spot for me. I hoped it was the hotspot for her, too. As I ran my tongue over her clit, I kept moving my fingers in and out of her pussy. She let out several moans and I hoped she wasn't faking it. I wanted to get her off, but women were notorious for faking it so it left me wondering. I kept at it and kept at it. Working a pussy was so much harder than working a cock and my tongue was starting to get tired. I was getting to the point where I was ready to give up when I felt her pussy get real tight and then pulsate in orgasm. I wasn't turned on by her coming; instead, I was totally intrigued at being face-to-face with a pussy as it came.

After relaxing for a few moments, Olivia sat up and pulled me in for a kiss. She said, "I love tasting myself on your lips, but now I want to taste you on your pussy's lips."

I was turned on by her words and excited for what was about to come. Olivia told me to get on all fours and then crawled up behind me. She licked my asshole a little bit before moving down and licking the lips of my pussy. After several minutes of teasing, she put her mouth on my clit and began sucking. It felt amazing, but all I could think was: *Darn it, I forgot about suction on the clit and how great it feels*. I should have done that to her. I told myself to stop thinking about the could've, would've, should've's and to enjoy the moment of losing my girl-on-girl virginity.

Olivia continued sucking on my clit from behind and I could feel the cum slowly seeping out of my pussy. Moments later, I felt her push two fingers into my pussy. I began moaning. Even though I preferred the roughness, I was enjoying her slow and gentle moves. I could feel my pussy tightening up, preparing for orgasm, when she moved her tongue off my clit and onto my asshole. The sensation of orgasm moved away and I didn't want to lose it so I said, "Put your lips back on my clit."

She did as I said and moments later I orgasmed. It wasn't a hard, deep orgasm, but a good orgasm; one similar to those when I masturbated with my vibrator. I crashed down on the bed and Olivia crawled up to lay next to me. She ran her fingers up and down my back gently as I recovered from my orgasm. After several minutes of silence, she asked, "Was that your first girl-on-girl experience?"

I responded, "Technically, yes."

She asked, "What did you think?"

I said, "I'm not really sure. I think I am taking it all in still."

We talked for a few more minutes and then Olivia pulled me in and cuddled me from behind. It was weird feeling her tits on my back. I had enjoyed the newness and excitement of our sexual experience, but cuddling felt very uncomfortable. *Was she expecting to stay the night?* Oh my God, I was acting like a man; I wanted her to leave after I fucked her. I couldn't do that to her. I was okay with her sleeping in the same bed as me; I had slept in the same bed as a woman many times before, but I wasn't fond of cuddling with one. It felt strange. She was so small and gentle. I loved cuddling when a man could hold me and give me a feeling of protection.

I lay for over an hour, thinking about this first sexual experience with a woman. I couldn't sleep. I felt like I had done something I had always wanted to try, but I also felt a sense of disappointment. As I stared at the wall, I felt the same feelings I'd felt the night I'd lost my virginity. I lay trying to understand everything that had just gone down, when I realized I had to be up in two hours for an interview. I decided to clear my mind and allow myself to fall asleep.

After Los Angeles, Steven and I made a stop in San Diego and then another stop in Phoenix. From there, we got to go home for a couple of days before heading to New York. Luckily, I only had two interviews while I was home so I had some time to relax and catch up with Nikki and Bree. We met for dinner at Nellcôte one night and after a couple of glasses of wine, I decided to tell them about my girl-on-girl experience in Los Angeles. Bree seemed taken aback by my words because she had never had a lesbian experience, but Nikki said, "It's about fucking time."

I tried to explain to them my feelings about it all, but Nikki told me I was overthinking it and that the next experience with a woman would be even better. I didn't think I wanted another experience with a woman. Sure, it was good, but it wasn't something that wowed me. Not only did I like the control and masculinity of a man, but I loved the sensation of a man penetrating me with his cock. Nikki told me I had to give it at least one more go because a person's first time was always awkward and uncomfortable. In the moment I had to agree with Nikki because if I had given up after I'd lost my virginity to a man, well, then I would've missed out on some great sexual experiences.

After telling Nikki and Bree about my

sexual experience, I told them about what had happened with Chase. I hadn't talked to either of them since the night before Thanksgiving because I had been with my family and then traveling. After telling the whole story, Nikki called Chase a "loony" because he believed he was an Indigo Child. When I told them about his group relationship, Bree said she had heard he was in a group relationship and her only reaction was that an ex who gets into a group relationship is the best scenario for any woman. I asked, "Why is it a good scenario?

Bree said, "Think about it."

I asked, "Think about what?"

Bree responded, "One woman is unable to satisfy him like you did so he had to get two women."

I said, "I guess, but he broke up with me because I couldn't satisfy him relationship-wise."

Nikki chimed in and said, "No woman will ever be able to satisfy that man relationship-wise. He's fucking crazy. Until he quits pretending to be secure with himself and actually becomes secure with himself, he's just going to blow through women." Nikki went on to ask, "Right, Bree?"

Bree said, "Nikki, there is some truth in what you say, but I'd have to have a few sessions with Chase before I could determine if he was actually crazy."

Nikki said, "Quit being so fucking professional, Bree. You know he's wacko."

Bree said, "I never said that. You said that."

I decided it was time to move on from this talk and said, "So, moving on…"

We moved on and discussed all the happenings with Nikki and Bree. After catching up with their lives, we headed home. Ben called while I was at dinner so I called him back during my cab ride home. He had bad news; he had to head to London for a few days so he wouldn't be in New York while I was there for interviews and book signings. While we were talking about why he had to go to London, Steven called me four times. I told Ben that something must be up so I had to call him back. I got off the phone with Ben and the moment I hung up, my phone was ringing again. It was Steven. I said, "Hello."

Steven screamed into the phone, "Darling, you are booked to be on Good Morning America Thursday!"

I said, "Shut the fuck up."

Steven said, "I told you to start watching your language."

"Seriously, Steven, I am going to be on Good Morning America?"

"Yes, darling, so we need to get you a killer outfit. Be at Akira tomorrow morning at 8am so they can get you something new to wear. We'll leave for the airport straight from there."

I woke up bright and early to meet Steven at Akira. They dressed me up and we were on our way to the airport. I was getting sick of flying, but the good thing about it was that it gave me time to write blog posts. Once in New York, it seemed like we were all over the place. There wasn't a moment to rest and by Wednesday night I was exhausted. I ended up going to bed at 7 p.m., which was good because I had to be up at 4 a.m. to be on Good Morning

America. I was excited to meet Robin Roberts and George Stephanopoulos, and be interviewed by Lara Spencer, but I'm pretty sure my mother was even more excited. She kept texting me for a play-by-play of my experience in the GMA studio.

I could feel my hands shaking when the producer sat me down while I waited for Lara to come over and interview me. I had been nervous with other interviews, but this one had my heart beating out of my chest. This was my first national TV appearance where millions would be watching. I wished I had taken a few shots of liquor before I sat down because I needed to calm the fuck down.

Lara came over and sat on the chair next to me. She looked at me and said, "Audrey, it's going to be okay, just breathe."

My face must've looked pale. I took a few deep breaths and once Ginger Zee was finished talking about the snow across the country, the cameraman looked at us and gave Lara a hand signal. That's when the interview began. I don't remember any of the questions I was asked until the last one when Lara said, "Rumor has it there is already a movie deal in the works. Is that rumor true?"

I didn't know what to say. I hadn't signed the contract yet. I looked over at Steven, who was standing behind the camera, and he threw his hands up like he didn't even know how to answer that question. I simply said, "If there is, I hope Mila Kunis plays me in the movie."

Lara said, "Great pick. She would be a perfect fit to play you in the movie," before she looked into the camera and continued, "That's all for our interview with Audrey Buchanan. Make sure to check out her new memoir *Dating Chase Walker*. We'll be right back after this commercial break."

Once the camera was off us, I felt my body relax before I stood up to give Lara a hug while thanking her for interviewing me. I took some photos to post on social media and send to my mom before I left. Then I made Steven go have brunch with me. I needed a mimosa after that interview. During brunch Chase texted me saying, "Congrats on the movie. I'm looking forward to you sending me a check for fifty percent."

I showed Steven the text and he told me to ignore it. I did as he said then I stuffed my face and drank two mimosas before we went back to the hotel to take naps. I had one more interview that evening.

After our naps and my interview with a local radio station, Steven invited me along to dinner with his friends. I felt special because Steven had never invited me out before. His friends were an absolute riot and as we ate dinner, I realized I really needed some more gay friends in my life. They were always so fun. We ate at Salinas and then headed to one of his friend's lofts. It was absolutely stunning with killer views of the city. I could stand in the window watching the snow come down over New York all night. I actually did do that for several minutes until Steven pulled me away from the window to introduce me to his friend. He said, "Audrey, this is Angelo. He is going to help you get on the *Chelsea Handler Show*."

I asked, "Really? Chelsea Handler? She is

an idol of mine."

Angelo said, "My goodness, Audrey, you are just a doll! You remind me of Audrey Hepburn."

I smiled and said, "That is a huge compliment. *Breakfast at Tiffany's* is one of my favorite movies."

Angelo clapped his hands together and said, "Mine too!"

Angelo and I took a seat on the couch and we talked about Audrey Hepburn's role as Holly Golightly for quite a while. I'm pretty sure he was the only person in the world who knew the movie better than me. We ended up discussing several of our favorite classic movies until Steven came over and said, "I'm feeling good and sexy. Let's go party somewhere!"

I had never seen Steven drunk so it was awesome seeing him letting loose and not barking orders at me. I asked, "Can we go to The Box? I love that place!"

Angelo asked, "How do you know about The Box?"

I said, "I went there last time I was in New York. Please, can we go?"

Angelo said, "Steven, what Miss Audrey Buchanan wants, Miss Audrey Buchanan gets. Let's go to The Box."

I stood up and let out a little cheer. Angelo got on his phone to reserve us a table and I went to the bathroom before we headed out of the door. I couldn't believe how quickly they had a limousine out front to pick us up. One of the guys popped open a bottle of champagne in the limo and then we cheered to a fun night out. It was almost 1am, but our night seemed to just be starting. We walked inside and got seated at our table. I was feeling buzzed from all the liquor I had consumed, but nowhere near as drunk as the men surrounding me. I decided to chug down my champagne and take a shot to catch up. Three glasses of champagne and two shots in less than an hour and I was definitely caught up. Feeling good and drunk, I decided to wander around and people-watch. The Box was one of the best places for people-watching. During my wander, I spotted a very attractive man. I mean, hot. He looked like a grown-up version of Zac Efron. I decided to "accidentally" run into him to get his attention. I planned to walk by and give him a nudge before apologizing for hitting him, but as I was walking my toe stubbed on something and I fell on the grown-up version of Zac Efron from behind, literally tackling him to the ground. I stood up, completely embarrassed by my clumsiness.

I put my hand out to assist bogus Zac Efron up while I apologized for sacking him like a football player. When he got up, his entire front side was wet. His drink had spilled all over him. I apologized again, but he told me not to worry about it. I told him I'd get some napkins, but he said, "I'll just go to the bathroom and dry off." He continued by saying, "I'm Jake," as he put his hand out to shake mine.

As I shook Jake's hand I said, "I'm Audrey and again, I am so sorry."

Jake shook my hand as he said, "I'm going to go to the bathroom to dry off. I'll be right back."

I said, "Let me go with you and help you."

I followed Jake to the bathroom and since nobody was in there, I followed him inside. He took off his suit jacket and handed it to me to hold while he unbuttoned his shirt. When he took his shirt off, he had an amazing body. Fuck, was this guy hot. I watched him as he ran the water over his shirt to rinse off the red cranberry juice on it. I felt myself getting turned on watching him. I was such a little whore, always getting turned on by sexy men. The champagne and shots mingling in my belly told me to kiss Stranger Jake and I listened to them. I grabbed Jake's arm and turned him toward me before kissing him passionately. He kissed me back and I felt butterflies run through my body. After kissing me passionately for a few moments, Jake picked me up and walked us into a stall. He closed the door behind him and then pulled my panties off from under my dress.

Once my panties were off, I unzipped his pants and pulled his cock out through the opened hole in his pants. He pulled out his wallet and unwrapped a condom while I sucked on his cock until it was rock hard. Once hard, he turned my body around and penetrated my pussy from behind. Everything was happening so fast that my pussy wasn't that wet at first, but I could feel it getting wetter with each thrust he made inside me. Jake grabbed my boobs from behind and pulled my body in closer while he fucked me. I was so turned on by the excitement of it all. Knowing we could get caught at any time completely turned me on, and I released a quick but satisfying orgasm. Moments after my orgasm, while my pussy was still pulsating, I felt Jake orgasm inside me. After several twitches of his body, Jake pulled out. He stood catching his breath while I put my panties back on. After his breaths, he pulled the condom off and threw it in the toilet before flushing it down.

When Jake went to zip his pants back up, he laughed because my cum had gathered all over his pants around the zipper. He said, "Audrey, I guess you wanted to even out my pants with my shirt and get them wet, too."

I laughed and said, "I'm sorry."

Jake said, "I look like a mess."

I said, "The good thing is that it is really dark in this club so nobody will even notice."

Jake said, "I hope so."

Jake finished cleaning up and asked if he could buy me a drink. I insisted that I buy him a drink because I had spilled his. We walked to the bar and I bought Jake a drink. We watched the show on stage and got to know one another a little bit. He was being very sweet and considerate, but I was not expecting anything to come of this. After all, I had just fucked him in the bathroom moments after meeting him. It was nearing 4 a.m. when Angelo came over and asked if I wanted to go and have breakfast at Tiffany's with him. I told Angelo I would love to.

I gave Jake a hug and told him it had been great to meet him before I skipped out of The Box with Angelo and into the limousine. The limo took us to a bakery where we bought donuts and coffee. I couldn't wait to get to Tiffany's so I could eat my donut. We got out of the limousine and walked around Tiffany's while eating our donuts. Once we finished eating our donuts, Angelo played the song *Moon River* on his phone. He put his hand out and asked me to dance. I accepted and he twirled me around in the snow on Fifth Avenue. I laughed the whole time and when he asked me to be his fellow drifter, I accepted. I had found a very fun new Huckleberry friend. We must've looked like a pair of idiots out there, dancing drunk before five in the morning, but I didn't care. I was having breakfast at Tiffany's for the second time in a matter of months. Decades of me dreaming of this moment and here I was playing it out for the second time.

When I flew out of New York later that day, my hangover kicked in. It was fucking dreadful, too. Luckily, I would have a few days of rest at home before I had to fly back to Los Angeles on Tuesday. Rest is exactly what I did. While I was home, I lay in bed all day Saturday and Sunday, but on Monday I got bundled up to go and walk around State Street to see the holiday decorations. Christmas was getting close and I wasn't sure how long I'd be stuck in Los Angeles.

While I was checking out the windows at Macy's, I felt my phone vibrating in my pocket. I pulled it out of my pocket and looked at the caller ID, noticing it was Chase calling. I didn't want to answer so I let it go to voicemail. Chase called again and I again let it go to voicemail. On the third time, I decided to pick it up. I answered, "Hello, Chase."

Chase said, "Hello, Audrey. Did you get my text?"

I said, "Yes."

He asked, "Why didn't you respond? You know I hate being ignored."

I said, "I've been really busy."

Chase said, "I think we need to get together and talk financials and my rights with your book and movie."

I asked, "Why?" I was utterly confused by

this man. First, he didn't have time to read my story, then he'd said 'fuck you' to me for exposing his life, then he came over and said he loved the story, and now that he'd found out there was a movie deal, he wanted in.

Chase sternly asked, "You don't think I'm owed anything? You are making a career and fortune off of exposing my life."

"Chase, when I sent you the manuscript you said you didn't care and you signed away your rights to the book. Now, all of a sudden, you care?"

"Yes, I do care and I think we should meet this week and come up with something fair. I may have signed away any rights to your book because I thought it would be another failure of a story of yours, but I never signed away rights to a movie deal."

Ouch, another failure of a story. What an asshole. I said, "I can't, Chase. I'm leaving for Los Angeles tomorrow."

Chase asked, "What are you doing right now?"

I said, "Looking at the Christmas decorations on State Street."

"Come by when you are finished. I'll be home in twenty minutes."

"Chase, that's not a good idea."

"Audrey, please come by after you are finished. That is all I will say. I look forward to seeing you."

My excitement for the Christmas decorations came to a screeching halt after talking to Chase and all I could think about was whether I should go to Chase's place to talk to him. The logical part of my brain said to call my lawyer and have him handle things, but the illogical part of my brain said that Chase and I could have a nice conversation about things and get it settled. I'd known this moment would come and deep down I think I had hoped for it. I finished looking at Macy's holiday-decorated windows before walking over to Starbucks to get a hot chocolate. After getting my hot chocolate, I decided to walk over to Chase's condo.

I signed in at the front desk and they called up. Chase granted me access. In the elevator my stomach felt uneasy from nerves. I kept telling myself not to let Chase twist my mind or allow him to pull any of his new-found voodoo crap on me. I would go in, keep my coat on, and simply listen to what he had to say.

I knocked on Chase's door and he opened it up before he said, "I knew you would come."

I said, "I can't stay long, but I wanted to hear what you have to say."

"Come in, take your coat off and let's chat. Do you want a glass of wine?"

I said, "No," and I am pretty sure that that was one of the only times I have ever turned down wine in my life. I was being strong.

In a tone that almost sounded like he was trying to woo me, Chase said, "Come on in, Audrey."

With irritation I said, "Chase, I told you, I can't stay. What is it that you want?"

"You look beautiful, Audrey."

"Cut it, Chase. What do you want?"

Chase asked in his sly voice, "Can't I just tell you that you look beautiful?"

I said, "No, now cut to the chase, Chase!"

"I want fifty percent of book sales, fifty percent of the movie, all rights to Chase Walker merchandising, to go on the rest of your book tour with you..."

I interrupted Chase and said, "You have to be fucking kidding me."

Chase pointed his finger at me as he said, "Don't interrupt me. You know I don't like that. There's more, I want you to be my number three."

I asked, "Your number three? What the fuck are you talking about?"

Chase grabbed my hand lightly and said, "I want you to join my group relationship. Your name is everywhere right now and our reality show will get picked up by a network for sure if you are involved."

I pulled my hand away from Chase and said, "Get the fuck out of here. First off, I am nobody's number three and second off, you can talk to my lawyer from here on. You are nutty, boy. What happened to you?"

"What happened to me? What happened to you? You took my life, exposed it and made a fucking career out of it."

I yelled, "I've given you tons of publicity, Chase!"

Chase yelled back, "Without my permission!"

I continued to yell, "I asked you for your permission and you didn't have time to read my story. I'll get you a fair deal, but you know what? I don't have time for this nonsense. I'm out. Find yourself another number three."

I marched out of Chase's condo and I was once again completely disturbed by my interaction with him. This guy was so fucking confusing. He said he was changing the way people love and didn't care about my story, yet he was demanding money from me. And as for me being his number three to score a reality show - what the hell? He'd broken up with me because he said he needed to be single during his reality show and now he wanted me in his group relationship to get picked up by a network? While this was all running through my head, I continued marching to the elevator. I heard my phone buzz so I pulled it out of my purse and saw it was a text from Ben asking, "Are you really busy or just ignoring me these days?" followed by a smiley face emoticon.

I responded, "No, I'm sorry, just a crazy day. I'll call you later."

When I got out of the Trump Building, I immediately called my lawyer, Phil. I told him about the series of events that had just gone down and Phil said that I could no longer communicate with Chase going forward and that he would take care of everything. He went on to say he was finalizing the movie deal and it would be ready for my signature when I landed in Los Angeles the next day.

The next day I got up and headed to the airport. Steven decided to stay in New York for a few extra days so he would be meeting me in Los Angeles. I was sort of relieved not to have to worry about him breathing over my shoulder the whole flight there, but I was even more grateful when I saw a super sexy man in the seat next to mine on the airplane.

I smiled at the super sexy guy before I sat down and then once seated I slowly took in his manly scent. I looked over at him out of the corner of my eye. Dark hair, dark skin, and built like a fucking rock. My pussy was jumping inside my panties telling me to jump on top of him. Fuck, I had to be the horniest girl that ever existed. Once my stuff was all arranged under my seat, I went to turn my phone off and noticed a text from Ben saying, "Hey, busy girl. Have a safe trip."

Fuck, I'd forgotten to call him back the night before. I was about to text Ben back to apologize when the flight attendant said, "Dear, you need to shut down all electronic devices."

The super sexy guy next to me said, "I think you're in trouble."

I laughed and turned my phone off without texting Ben back. I'd text him as soon as I landed in Los Angeles. Once my phone was in my bag, I sat back in my seat. I couldn't use electronic devices, nor did I have a magazine, so I just sat there in silence. The hot, hairy, and good-smelling man next to me was looking out of the window in silence so I decided to spark up a conversation. I asked, "Do you live in Chicago?"

Hot, hairy, and good-smelling man responded, "I do. Do you?"

I said, "Yes, I'm headed to Los Angeles on business."

Hot, hairy, and good-smelling man said, "Me too. I'm actually only there for a few hours. I have to fly back to Chicago later today."

I said, "That's a lot of flying for one day."

Hot, hairy, and good-smelling man said, "Yeah, I shouldn't even be leaving for the day, but it's business."

I asked, "What part of Chicago do you live in?"

"I'm near River North, on the river."

I said, "I'm in Wicker Park."

Hot, hairy, and good-smelling man said, "Oh yes, the artsy part of town."

I asked, "What's your name?"

Hot, hairy, and good-smelling man looked a little confused, but then responded, "I'm 'G.'"

I put my hand out to shake his and said, "Well, I'm 'A,' nice to meet you."

'G' and I continued talking for quite a while. I liked the mystery of us not revealing our names. It was fun and, my God, just watching this guy's mannerisms turned me on. I could literally feel myself moving into uncomfortable horniness. I kept adjusting myself in the seat and re-crossing my legs. It was ridiculous for any girl to feel this horny; I'm pretty sure my female parts functioned more like a male's. Even though I didn't have a boner to hide, I had to keep shifting because I could feel my panties gathering cum and certain positions sent way too many butterflies through my pussy.

'G' and I chatted for a good hour. He didn't give me much insight into himself because he was very intrigued to find out about me. At one point, 'G' bit his lip and he looked even sexier. I couldn't take it anymore so I excused myself and went into the restroom. When I got in there, I pulled my pants down and masturbated really quickly. I came in no time. I wiped the cum off my pussy and out of my panties before I washed my hands and headed back to my seat. As I was walking back to my seat, I began wondering if there was something wrong with me - I'm sure men have jacked off in airplane restrooms many times before, but a woman?

I was more relaxed when I sat back in my seat because I got that little orgasm out, but 'G' had his eyes closed and looked like he was resting. I pulled my computer out and decided to work on some blog posts. After my recent encounter with Chase and his request for me to be his number three in his group relationship, I decided writing a post about group relationships could be interesting. Maybe really thinking about it might help me understand why people decide to participate in group relationships.

I wrote and wrote, but by the end I decided I still deserved to be a man's number one instead of his number three. While I was finishing up, 'G' said, "Interesting article you are writing there."

I said, "I thought you were sleeping and here you are creeping on my work."

'G' said, "I just opened my eyes a few minutes ago."

I said, "Sure you did."

"No, really I did. So, do you always write about sex and relationships?"

I said, "No..." but before I was able to finish explaining myself a kid came up and asked, "Can I get your autograph?"

I knew this kid couldn't be talking to me so I looked at 'G' and he said to the kid, "Of course. Who should I make it out to?"

The kid responded, "Matt, please."

'G' signed the napkin with his autograph and then gave the kid a high-five before he walked away with excitement. I looked at 'G' and asked, "Who are you? Should I know who you are or something?"

'G' responded, "I told you, I'm 'G.'"

I said, "Okay, 'G'"

'G' said, "Now, back to my question; do you only write dirty things?"

'G' and I chatted until the plane landed in Los Angeles. While the plane was taxiing, 'G' asked for my phone. He put his number in under the name 'G' and told me to give him a call when I got back to Chicago. I was intrigued, that's for sure. We hugged goodbye at the gate and 'G' said he looked forward to hearing from me.

A car picked me up at LAX and took me to the hotel. I checked in and changed before meeting my lawyer, Phil, downstairs for a lunch meeting. Phil was already there waiting for me when I arrived. I said hello as I approached the table and as I was sitting down, Phil said, "Guess who's suing you?"

I said, "Hmm, let me guess. Chase?"

Phil responded, "Bingo. Don't worry, I have it all under control."

I said, "I know he wants fifty percent, but tell him he can have twenty-five percent."

"No, Audrey. I can work this so he gets nothing."

"Phil, I wouldn't have a story if I had never met Chase. I found myself sexually when I was with him and he is Chase Walker so he believes he deserves 'a cut,'" I used air quotes, "of whatever something someone around him is doing. How do you think he's made his money? He sets things up and then rides the wave. The sooner we cut a deal, the sooner I can get back to moving on."

"I don't recommend this, Audrey."

I said, "I know, Phil, but this is what I want." Then I asked, "What's next?"

Phil said with seriousness, "The private investigator found out who vandalized your car."

Not knowing there was an investigation outside of the police, I asked, "Who hired a private investigator?"

Phil said, "Your father and your agent thought it was a good idea."

I asked, "Shouldn't I have been advised about this?"

Phil said, "There was nothing you could do about it anyway."

I said, "Still, I think I should be the one deciding stuff like this."

"Well, the girl who vandalized your car is named Vivian Voss."

When I heard the name Vivian I suddenly realized I had seen that name recently. I said, "Wait, that girl tweeted me something recently."

Phil said, "Yes, we know, and she happens to be your ex's new girlfriend."

It was like a light bulb went on in my head suddenly. I said, "Oh yeah, I saw the name Vivian on Chase's phone."

Phil shook his head back and forth as he said, "Audrey, you should not be around that guy anymore. Communication with him should go through me."

I knew I shouldn't have been talking to Chase, but I still made up an excuse by saying, "I know, but he shows up at my place randomly."

Phil said, "I think we should get a restraining order against both of them."

"What? A restraining order? Chase is harmless. He's just in a strange spiritual phase in his life."

Phil said with a sense of disappointment in his voice, "His girlfriend vandalized your car, Audrey."

I said, "I know, but he's got some group relationship going where they are going to be rid of jealousy. I'm sure in a couple weeks she'll be all caught up in his world and under his spell."

Phil asked, "Audrey, what are you talking about?"

I said, "Never mind, but there's no need for a restraining order right now. Let's move on. What's next on the agenda?"

Phil shook his head again in disappointment before he said, "The movie contract is ready to be signed."

I smiled as I said, "Oh, yeah? Sum it up for me."

"You are selling the movie rights for $1.3 million and you will own twenty percent."

I shouted, "Shut the front door, Phil!"

Phil looked at me with confusion and asked, "What?"

I said, "It's an expression. The clean way of saying 'Shut the fuck up.'"

"Oh, I see. Does that mean you are happy with the deal?"

"Fuck, yeah, Phil. That's ridiculous!"

Phil pulled out a pile of papers and said, "Take this contract up with you after lunch and read it word for word. We have a meeting at the production company's office tomorrow to sign."

I asked, "Phil, do I really have to read this?"

"Yes, Audrey, you do."

"Can you send a copy to my father, too? Just so I have another set of eyes, you know."

"I already sent him a copy this morning, but you still have to read it."

I said, "Yes, sir."

Phil and I finished lunch. I tried to get him to loosen up, but it wasn't easy. When I left, I went to my room, sat on my bed, and started to read the contract. It was way too much mumbo jumbo for my liking so I texted my dad and asked what he thought of the contract. He responded, "Fair. I support it one hundred percent."

I responded, asking, "So I should sign it?"

My father replied, "I think you need to read it before you decide if you are going to sign it."

I lied and told my father I was going to read it. I knew I wouldn't, though. I trusted my father and if he said it was good, well, that was good enough for me. Instead of using my free time to read a life-changing contract, I decided to finally call Ben back. When he answered he asked, "How are you, Miss Celebrity?"

I said, "I'm exhausted. How is New York?"

He said, "Things are good here. Do you think you'd be able to come out here for New Year's?"

I had always wanted to go to New York to watch the ball drop on New Year's, so I said, "I think I can make that work."

With enthusiasm Ben said, "Great, we'll go

to the Ritz Carlton for dinner and then I have a room at the Renaissance Hotel where we can watch the ball drop."

I asked, "Really? We can see the ball drop from the hotel room?"

Ben said, "Really, unless you prefer to deal with the crowds on the streets?"

I said, "No, I mean I don't mind where we watch it from as long as I can see it, but I didn't know we could watch it from a hotel room."

Ben said, "I actually reserved this room two years ago so even if you said you didn't want to watch it from in there, well, I'd work really hard to change your mind."

I asked, "You seriously booked this room two years ago?"

Ben said, "Even when you have a lot of money, it is still hard to get a room that overlooks the ball dropping on New Year's Eve."

I said, "I bet. I'll book a flight when I get back to Chicago."

Ben responded, "No, I'll take care of it. You know that I love taking care of you."

I said, "Ben, I can buy my own ticket. I'm signing my movie deal tomorrow for $1.3 million dollars!"

"Wow, nice work, but I still want to buy your ticket."

"Fine, but next time you come to Chicago, it's on me!"

Ben and I talked a little longer. He was really pushing for us to try to spend more time together. I did like him, but I kept telling myself I needed more time to get over the whirlwind of a relationship I just had with Chase. I knew Ben was nothing like Chase, but I still had a lot to learn about him. Plus, if Ben and I did date, it would bring big changes for both of us since he lived in New York and I lived in Chicago. I had so much going on already that I felt I needed some more time just worrying about me.

I interviewed with Chelsea Handler and it was my favorite interview to date; partly because there was plenty of vodka to drink in the green room prior to my interview, but mostly because she's hilarious and a writer I've always admired. After my interview, I met my lawyer Phil and the production company to sign my movie deal. It all seemed so surreal that a whirlwind sexual romance of mine had turned into writing a get-over-him vomiting of words, into a published memoir, and now into a movie. My life had changed so much in a matter of months. My father consistently referred to this period in my life as "time for Audrey Buchanan" and I was loving every moment of it.

After a few days with my crazy family for Christmas, I was off to New York City for New Year's with Ben. I was ecstatic to finally be there to see the ball drop in Times Square in person. For so many years, it had just been something I'd excitedly wait to see on my TV screen and now I'd be watching it from the window of a fancy hotel room. I'm not sure where all my luck with well-off men had come from in the past several months, but I wasn't about to start complaining.

The evening I landed in New York, Ben and I stayed in and ordered pizza. Being from Chicago, I wasn't a fan of New York pizza, but he loved it so I ate it. We drank some wine and built a fort in the living room near the fireplace like we were kids. It was fun and I hadn't laughed like that in years. Ben was telling me a story from his childhood about when he played 'hot lava' with his sister and while he was telling me he had a huge smile on his face. It was endearing, seeing him so tickled about his past, and in a strange way, it turned me on. I leaned over and kissed him mid-story. Ben kissed me back. We kissed passionately for several minutes before his hand began caressing my breasts from over my shirt and bra. Ben then pulled my shirt off over my head and I assisted him in taking his shirt off. We went back to kissing, shirtless, for a few more minutes before Ben unbuttoned my pants. Trying to pull my pants off in the small space of the couch cushion and blanket fort we had built wasn't easy. Somehow Ben managed, though. When it comes to sex, no matter the obstacle, a man will find a way to make it happen.

Instead of taking his pants off, Ben just unzipped them and pulled them down a little before moving on top of me and penetrating his cock in my pussy. I moaned in pleasure with the initial penetration. Ben moved his cock in and out of my pussy, slowly, as I felt myself getting more wet with each thrust. My God, I loved sex; lying there, so warm underneath him, made me feel a mix of comfort, safety, warmth, and turned on. As Ben increased speed, I closed my eyes and enjoyed the feeling of my pussy tightening up with each thrust. However, the moment I started really getting into it, Ben pulled out and came on my stomach. Even before the cum had finished spitting out of Ben's cock, he said, "I am so sorry!"

I looked at him and smiled before I said, "It's okay. Don't be sorry. I take it as a huge compliment."

Ben looked at me and said, "No, I am sorry. It won't happen again. I just haven't masturbated in quite some time so I couldn't hold back."

I said, "Ben, I totally understand. It's no big deal."

Ben said, "It is a big deal. I want to get you off. Give me two minutes and I'll be ready to go again."

"Ben, it's okay. I'm here for three days so

I'm sure we will have sex plenty of times. Lie down, relax, and enjoy coming down from your orgasm."

We lay in the fort for a few minutes quietly. I cuddled up to Ben and rubbed my hands gently around his hairy chest. I was enjoying the quiet comfortableness of being cuddled up with Ben in our quaint little fort. I could feel my body relaxing and I probably could have fallen asleep in a matter of minutes, but suddenly Ben rolled on top of me before standing up and busting up our fort like he was the Kool-Aid man, yelling out, "Oh yeah!" or something. After Ben had busted open our cushion walls, he got down on his knees and wrapped his arms around my legs. He pulled my body close and then wrapped his lips around my pussy. He moved his tongue around my labia slowly, which brought my body back into relaxation mode. I closed my eyes and took in each movement of his tongue.

Several minutes passed before he inserted his finger in my pussy. I moaned in pleasure. He moved his finger in and out. It didn't feel bad, but it didn't feel good. It felt like he was poking me and it was making me lose my clit hard-on with each poke. I closed my eyes and tried to think of a way to redirect him because this poking was completely unacceptable. I decided to put my hand down on his to pull his poking finger out of my pussy. As I was doing so, Ben said, "Oh, so you want me to fuck you?"

Well, Ben thinking that he wasn't completely failing fingering me and thinking I just wanted to be fucked worked and I was glad I hadn't hurt his feelings. Ben stuck his cock inside my pussy with force and moved in deep for a few moments. I closed my eyes to take in the sensation, but it didn't last long because all of a sudden Ben pulled out and came on my stomach. As I felt the little squirts of jizz hitting my stomach I heard Ben say, "Fucking A!"

I opened my eyes, but I didn't say anything at first. After Ben had finished coming he lay down next to me. I said, "Two compliments in one night. You are so sweet," before I leaned over and kissed him on the cheek.

Ben said, "I don't know what is going on! You know I can last longer, right? Remember when I was in Chicago? We had sex for a long time. I assure you, this is unusual."

I said, "Ben, don't worry about it. I'm not questioning your manhood."

Ben said with aggravation, "I just don't know why this happened... twice!"

I joked as I said, "I bet it's that damn New York pizza."

Ben laughed as he said, "If so, I'm going to be only eating Chicago pizza from here on."

I said, "Good, that's how it should be."

Ben suggested, "Let's go clean up and cuddle in bed. You can pick the movie."

Ben and I cuddled up in bed. I picked *When Harry Met Sally* for the movie. Ben said it was a good pick, yet he was snoring before Harry and Sally had even made it to the orgasmic diner scene. I thought that Sally's loud fake orgasm might wake Ben up, but he was out cold. I watched the entire movie and then turned the TV off. I lay in bed in the dark for a little while, but I couldn't sleep. Something was on my mind, bothering me. I knew that feeling all too well, but I couldn't figure out what was bothering me. Everything seemed to be going so well for me.

I quietly got out of bed and walked into the kitchen. I poured myself a glass of wine and then sat next to the window. I looked outside at all of the lights and buildings thinking about how there were so many people out there, just living. I thought about how the year was coming to an end and wondered what the new year would bring. I sat there wondering so many things for quite some time, but they were all just thoughts and those thoughts were keeping me awake. I needed to get the thoughts out. I needed to figure out why my mind was restless. I walked away from the window and pulled out my laptop. I curled up on the couch with a big, fluffy blanket and I started writing.

Words were pouring out of me. The storyline: an aspiring actress moves to New York City from a small town, sleeping her way to the top. I was immersed in the story and before I knew it the sun was coming up and I had written just over seven thousand words. After noticing that night had turned into morning, I decided it was time to get some sleep. I closed my laptop and went into Ben's bedroom to crawl back into bed with him. He pulled me in and held me tight. Ben's warm embrace was so comfortable that I was asleep in a matter of seconds.

Around noon, Ben woke me up with a kiss on my forehead. It put a smile on my face and set my mood for the day as super positive. Once my eyes were open, Ben smiled at me and said it was time to get up because we had a big day ahead. He was already showered and dressed for the day, and he smelled so good. I rubbed my eyes and then stretched my arms over my head as I asked how much time I had to get ready. He said I had about an hour before we had lunch reservations. After lunch, we would be heading to Bloomingdales to get a new dress and suit for the night. I said, "Ben, you like shopping more than most girls. Are you gay?"

Ben laughed and said, "I like shopping because I like spoiling you. Come on, it'll be fun. My personal shopper has already pulled items for us."

I jokingly said, "I guess I'll go spend the day shopping."

Ben and I had a light lunch and then went shopping before checking into the Renaissance Hotel to get ready for dinner. The view of Times Square was amazing. I didn't even want to go to dinner, but we had early reservations so we'd be back in our room by 10pm. Heading to dinner, there were so many crowds of people that I worried we wouldn't be able to get back. I questioned Ben about whether we should go to the Ritz for dinner or if we should stay at the Renaissance. Ben assured me we'd be back with plenty of time to relax before the ball dropped at midnight.

Dinner at the Ritz was pretty fucking amazing, so I'm glad we went, but the journey back to the Renaissance wasn't easy. We did most of it by foot so I was damn glad there wasn't much snow on the ground to trek through in my heels. Once in our room, I kicked those heels off fast and then started jumping on the bed. Ben laughed at me and then joined me.

I couldn't jump long because my dinner was jumping around in my stomach so I slowed down and the moment I slowed down Ben pulled me close to him and kissed me. As our lips locked, Ben wrapped his arms around me and unzipped my dress. It dropped down around my ankles.

I worked my hands down his chest, unbuttoning each button on his shirt. After I'd unbuttoned the last button, I pulled his shirt off him and down his arms. His hairy, muscular chest was so manly and sexy that it was an instant turn-on. I put my hands on his belt buckle next and unzipped his pants. Once his pants had dropped down around his ankles, I nibbled on his lip before moving my lips down the front of his body. I stopped on his cock where I licked it like it was a popsicle; spending time only licking the top and then pushing it deep down my throat. I placed my right hand down on his shaft and twisted it around as I continued filling my mouth with his cock. I heard him moan in pleasure and I felt his cock get harder with each twist I made with my hand.

I looked up and smiled at Ben. He smiled back as he said, "I have to be inside of you right now. I want to feel the inside of your wet pussy."

I was a little surprised he wanted to get his cock in my pussy so fast after our last two sessions with his premature ejaculation, but I liked seeing his demanding side. I stood up on the bed and said, "What the fuck are you waiting for? Put your cock inside of my pussy!"

Still standing on the bed, Ben spun my body

around and I placed my hands on the wall above the headboard. He put his cock inside my pussy with force and it felt amazing. He grabbed my hips and used them to quickly push his cock in and out of me. The force and the control were a huge turn-on and I felt my pussy getting tighter with each thrust. I didn't want him to cum before I came so I let the orgasm build up and then I released it with a loud screamish moan. The moment I felt my pussy begin to relax after its tense orgasm explosion, I felt Ben pull his cock out of my pussy and cum on my ass.

We spent several minutes catching our breaths and taking in the euphoria from our orgasms. I looked over at Ben and I could see him in a happy glow of a trance while he embraced his orgasm. Looking at him made my heart smile. While I was watching Ben with a smiling heart, there was a knock on the door. Ben got up real fast and grabbed two robes out of the closet. He threw one at me and told me to put it on.

Once I was covered by the soft, comfy white robe, Ben opened the door to our room and welcomed the room service guy in. He walked in with a cart full of desserts and champagne. It all looked delicious. Ben tipped the guy and as soon as he was out of the room, I threw my robe off and started jumping on the bed again with excitement. Ben laughed at me and said, "I could watch you jump up and down naked all day long."

I said, "Throw your robe off and join me!"

Ben said, "I'd rather just watch you, but okay, it looks like fun!"

Ben threw his robe off and starting jumping with me on the bed. He grabbed my hands and then we jumped in a circle. While we were jumping, I looked down and saw his flaccid dick bouncing around and I started laughing so hard I fell down. I had never seen a flaccid dick bouncing around like that. Ben's face got red with embarrassment and then he sat down next to me. I told him not to be embarrassed and that I thought it was cute. He jokingly said, "Whatever," before getting off the bed to pour us each a glass of champagne.

We stayed naked and pulled two chairs up by the window, watching all the hustle and bustle outside. While we watched, we talked about our hopes for the new year. Ben said he hoped this girl he was crushing on would want to get more serious in the new year and I joked with him, telling him good luck with that. I knew he was talking about me and I had never had as much fun with someone; nor had I ever felt more comfortable, but I felt scared inside whenever he talked about us 'giving it a go' with a relationship. I wasn't sure why I felt so scared and in need of more time. What kind of girl doesn't jump at the chance of settling down with a New York City playboy-turned-nice guy who is ready to settle down? Not only was he a nice guy, but he was funny and hot, really fucking hot. Oh, and really fucking rich, too. Seriously, something had to be wrong with me.

We talked each other's ears off until we had a long, passionate kiss at midnight. After we kissed, Ben pulled away, smiled at me and said, "Audrey, I love you."

It was a shocker; a pleasant shocker, not an

unpleasant shocker like when a guy puts his finger in your asshole with no warning. Even though it was a pleasant shocker, I didn't say it back. I wanted to, but I wasn't ready yet. I adored Ben like I had never adored a man before, but my insides were telling me I needed more time. I used sex to break the awkwardness of me not saying 'I love you' back to Ben when he'd said it to me. I started by rubbing his cock gently while we kissed. Once I could feel it growing in my hand, I reached down and caressed his balls. He moved his hands around my breasts before moving down to my pussy and tenderly playing with my labia. The gentleness didn't last long though, and soon Ben laid me down on the bed and penetrated my pussy. The initial penetration never, ever got old.

Ben fucked me slowly, missionary style, for a few minutes before he flipped me over on my stomach. I lifted up my hips and he penetrated my pussy from behind. He was fucking me deep and hard so I said, "Oh yeah, fuck me hard!"

Ben asked, "Do you like when I fuck you hard?"

I said, "I love when you fuck me hard."

"Do you want it deeper?"

"Yeah, fuck me harder and deeper."

Ben pushed his cock deeper inside me with each thrust. A couple of thrusts felt like he had hit the bottom of my lungs, taking my breath away with his cock. After a few quiet moments, Ben yelled out, "Do you want it harder, baby?"

Hearing Ben call me 'baby' sent a negative feeling through my body that felt like someone had punched me in the gut. I yelled out with force and seriousness while I pushed him off me, "Never, ever call me 'baby' again!"

When I looked at Ben, he was completely still. He didn't say a word and had a look of shock on his face. I burst into tears and said, "Oh, my God, I am so sorry. I didn't mean to yell at you like that."

Ben asked, "What just happened?"

I said, "Ben, truly, I am sorry."

"I know, Audrey. I know you aren't a mean person. I just need to know what that was all about."

"You calling me 'baby' sent a terrible feeling through my body."

Ben asked, "Why?"

I said, "I think it is because Chase always called me 'baby.'"

"Okay, fair enough. So no calling you 'baby.' I can handle that."

"I'm so sorry, Ben."

Ben gently said, "Audrey, don't sweat it. I understand."

I asked, "How do you understand?"

Ben lay down and put his head on the pillow. He signaled for me to lie next to him, so I did. I looked at him as he said, "I know you are still recovering from Chase. I understand that. I jumped into your life suddenly and quite strangely. Even I wonder why I sent that message to you one night and why I have a desire to just hug you all hours of the day. It's fucking strange." *Whoa, Ben just swore! He only swore during sex.* "Audrey, I want you. I want to be in Chicago with you. I want you here in New York with me. I just want to be around you all the time. I want the past couple hours of us talking about our separate hopes for the new year to be us talking about our hopes for the new year as a couple."

I was a little taken aback. I'd known Ben wanted a fairy tale with me, but I never realized how serious he was about it. I knew he was the type of person who saw what he wanted and went and got it. He never let anything or anyone stand in his way and that's how he'd made millions of dollars, but I have never been the 'eyes-on-the-prize' go-getter type.

We snuggled up and Ben fell asleep. He was breathing hard behind me for a few moments and then he began to snore. I listened to his snoring, trying to find a pattern to help me fall asleep, but he wasn't snoring in much of a pattern so I slowly snuck out of bed and took a seat in front of the window. There were still thousands of people wandering the streets. I decided to bundle up and go for a walk.

As I walked around watching drunk people wander the streets, I thought about why I was hesitant to let myself love Ben. Was it the distance? Was it that I knew he wanted to settle down? Was it that I was still recovering from Chase? Was it the lack of challenge? Was it that there was something missing between us? Was it all too fast and too much for me? For nearly an hour, I wandered the streets, only stopping to buy a pretzel from a street vendor, but during all that wandering, I couldn't figure out why I was so hesitant to 'give us a go', as Ben would say.

I got back to Chicago and it was snowing hard. I was surprised the airplane I was on was able to land. It took the town car that drove me home from the airport almost two hours to get me to my apartment, which was a drive that usually took about half an hour. Once I was home, I threw on my pajamas and I was ready to cuddle up under a blanket on my couch. Before I cuddled up, I went to pour myself a glass of wine and I noticed I was out of wine. *What a fucking crock*. I threw on a jacket and some boots and trudged through the snow to the grocery store to get some wine. I bought myself six bottles just because I didn't want to have to trudge through the snow again and because I found out I would save ten percent if I bought six bottles at a time.

Finally cuddled up on my couch, I took a look at the blinking cursor on my screen to get back to writing the story about a girl who slept her way up to fame in New York. I got into it fast. Words were pouring out of me at record speeds. Everyone in Chicago was snowed in and flights were getting cancelled left and right so Steven rescheduled our trip to Miami. The snow couldn't have come at a better time because I was ready to write and the inclement weather kept me at home.

While I was home writing away one night,

there was a knock on my door. I had a weird feeling it was Chase because he had texted me several times saying that he needed to talk to me, but I kept ignoring his texts and phone calls. I ran into my bedroom to hide. I have no idea why I thought I needed to run into my bedroom to hide because Chase couldn't see into my apartment, but I still proceeded. While I was hiding behind my bedroom door, the knocking stopped, but I waited a few moments before I walked out of my bedroom. As I was walking out of my bedroom I heard my front door opening. I thought: *What the fuck? Is someone breaking into my apartment?*

I ran into my bathroom and locked the door behind me. I was freaking out, thinking I was getting robbed. I got into the shower and quietly closed the shower curtain. Getting into the shower and closing the curtain was my extra layer of protection from the robbers. I stayed as quiet as I could as I heard someone walking around my apartment and all I kept thinking was: *Don't kill me. Please don't kill me.*

As I was making a million promises to God, assuring him I'd be a better person, I heard a man's voice say, "Audrey, I know you are home. There's a half-drank glass of wine, your computer's screensaver isn't on and your phone is here." *Fuck - it was Chase.*

As I stepped out from behind the shower curtain, I realized that I had never gotten my key back from Chase after we broke up. Why the fuck was he here? I opened my bathroom door and walked out of my bedroom into the living room. Chase was standing there, all bundled up in a jacket, hat and scarf. I said,

"Why are you here, Chase? I'm not supposed to be talking to you."

Chase said, "Audrey, you need to stop listening to what everyone else is telling you to do. You need to connect with your own mind and make decisions."

I said, "Chase, I've made the decision based on their suggestion. Now, you really need to leave."

Chase said, "I need to tell you something very important before I can leave."

I asked, "What, you are suing me for something else now?"

Chase said, "That money is rightfully mine and you know that. No, it doesn't have to do with money. God sent me here to talk to you."

I said, "Shut the front door, Chase."

Confused by my choice of words of 'shut the front door' rather than 'shut the fuck up,' Chase asked, "What?"

Apparently, I am the only person that uses this phrase, because my lawyer Phil didn't get it either. Instead of explaining my clean attempt at saying 'shut the fuck up,' I said, "Chase, leave and shut the front door on your way out."

Chase said, "I need to talk to you and I am not leaving until I give you God's message."

I said with irritation, "Crap, fine; let me refill my glass of wine first. Do you want a glass?"

Chase said, "Okay, I'll have a glass."

While I was filling up our glasses of wine, Chase took his coat off and sat down on the couch. I walked over and handed him his glass of wine before I curled up on the couch under my blanket. I said, "Alright Chase, tell me the word of the Lord."

Chase said, "I need you to stop joking and take me seriously. I am being one-hundred-percent serious that God has chosen me to deliver this message to you."

I was still shocked at how much Chase had changed since we'd broken up, so I said, "Alright, I'll get serious, but I need to ask you something first."

"What do you need to ask me?"

I asked with seriousness, "Are you on drugs?"

Chase gave me a look like he was offended by my question and said, "Audrey, no. I am not on drugs. Now, listen to what I have to say."

Chase told me that he had done a meditation a couple of days ago and in that meditation God had spoken to him. He'd brought Chase to a beautiful beach and that beach had been empty. Only God and Chase stood on that beach until Chase saw me walking toward him in a wedding dress. Chase said he had never seen me look more beautiful and happy in my life and in those moments of me walking toward him, he had never felt that type of happiness. Before I got close to Chase, God stopped me and tied me up to a tree. When Chase saw me tied to the tree, he said he felt pain and that God told him it was his way of showing Chase the pain he had caused me when he'd broken my heart.

The story continued and so did God's lesson to Chase. While I'd been tied to the tree, God had sent dozens of beautiful women onto the beach. All of these women were to belong to

Chase. Continuing on, Chase said that while I had been tied to the tree, God had taken the pain I was feeling inside, watching him with all these beautiful women, and put it inside Chase for him to feel for a few minutes. Chase said he had never realized just how badly he had hurt me until God had placed that pain inside him for a few minutes. I cut in here and asked, "Chase, is this really what you came to tell me?"

Chase began to cry and said, "Yes, but there's more."

I said, "Okay, let's get to the point here."

Chase wept hard, screaming out, "I am so sorry for hurting you," while he got up to come and hug me.

I responded as he hugged me, "Chase, it's fine. I'm good."

Chase said, "No, you aren't good. As I was speaking to God about why he'd put me through that pain, he told me more. You aren't going to be okay, Audrey. God told me that you aren't going to be able to have children of your own."

My jaw literally dropped. I wasn't sure how to respond so I yelled, "Out! Get the fuck out of my apartment right now before I call the police!"

"Audrey, listen to me. I am a messenger for God and you need to think about this and accept it."

As I walked toward the door I said, "I swear to fucking God, if you don't leave right now I am calling the police. Out! Now!"

Chase begged me to talk longer by saying, "Audrey, please!"

"Out, Chase, now!"

173

Chase finally got up and walked toward the door. As he was exiting he said, "Audrey, just know that I love you and I will continue sending you love from afar. Whenever you feel down, close your eyes and I assure you that you will be able to feel my loving energy."

I slammed the door in Chase's face while he was talking, but then opened it up and said, "Give me the key to my apartment, now!"

Chase continued mumbling about some crap as he took the key off his key ring. I wasn't paying attention as my only concern was getting the key to my apartment. Once Chase had given me the key, I slammed the door shut and locked it up. Locking him out was all I could do, but that boy needed to be locked inside of a loony bin. I walked back to my living room, sat on my couch and called Nikki. She was shocked by the story and agreed that Chase had lost it. She said he sounded like one of those crazy preachers who pulled you in and then stole all your money. I had to agree. I wasn't sure where the Chase I knew had gone, but every interaction I had with the new Chase made it easier and easier for me to move on.

I was loving all the time I had to spend inside because of the snow. I was in the mood to write and the snow kept everyone inside. I had to go to Miami for two days for radio interviews, a photo shoot, and book signings, but I was so busy there that time flew by. It felt good to see some sunshine, but they were the first interviews I'd done since Chase had started doing interviews of his own about the memoir. I probably should have listened to his interviews but I didn't, so I was a bit taken aback when I was asked how I felt about Chase leaving me to pursue a group relationship. It took me a few seconds to answer, but I took what Bree had said about it and responded, "It is the best situation any girl who's got her heart broken could be in; it means he can't find just one girl to satisfy him like I could."

The radio DJ laughed a little and agreed. I decided this was going to be my generic answer for this question going forward and hoped that no other interviews would pry much further. I had to start getting used to the fact that Chase was going to be out there doing interviews too, and telling his side of the story while promoting what he had going on. I had been so upset when he hadn't cared enough to read the damn story, but now that he was utilizing the exposure I was starting to wish he'd go back to not caring.

Once back in Chicago, I got back to hardcore writing. I was deep in my story and loving that I was completely inspired by myself and not needing someone to sexually inspire my words. This is what I needed. I needed to know that I could write something amazing without the inspiration or the heartache of a man.

It took just under two weeks between that night at Ben's when I had started writing the story until I finished the last word. I called Nikki up to tell her the good news and she said she'd missed me so much. She suggested we meet at the tavern between our apartments to celebrate. I was in. I threw on about ten layers of clothing and trudged through all the snow to walk to the bar. It was rather empty inside the bar when we arrived. Nikki and I took down shot after shot in celebration and caught up on each other's lives. I felt like we had been so distant from one another; and we had been, because of all my traveling.

Nikki was onto a new guy as usual so she told me all about him and I told her every last detail of my trip to New York for New Year's. Nikki said I should just let Ben in and give it a go. She said it would be awesome to be able to call New York and Chicago home. I loved being around Ben, but he was being rather distant since I'd left New York. We texted here and there; however, I was a little worried that me yelling at him for calling me 'baby' and me not saying 'I love you' back when he told me he loved me had pushed him away.

Talking about Ben made me want to talk to him so I texted Ben saying, "Hey," but he didn't respond right away like he usually did. Because I was pretty drunk, this had me even more worried. Nikki and I kept drinking and drinking. We drank to the point at which we should have stopped at least an hour prior. Nikki drunk-texted her new bald, tattooed piece of hotness and he ended up coming to the bar to join us. He brought a friend who was really annoying. I can't remember why his friend was so annoying, but he was. He was probably annoying to me because he was sober and I was drunk. Sober people don't usually mix well with drunk people. One of the parties is bound to get annoyed at some point.

I kept checking my phone every few minutes, hoping Ben would respond to my text, but he never did and with each additional shot of tequila I added to my belly, I began to feel angrier about Ben not responding, rather than feeling hurt or worried.

While I was getting upset about Ben not responding, Nikki decided to tell her new boy-toy the story of the guy 'G' that I had met on the plane on my way to Los Angeles. She wanted to see if he could help us figure out why this guy was famous. Being a drunk idiot, I decided to pull out my phone and text 'G.' I said, "Hey, sexy, it's 'A' from the plane."

A few minutes later 'G' texted back, "Hello, A. I thought you had forgotten about me."

I responded, "I did, until I started drinking tequila."

He asked, "So is this a booty call?"

I asked, "Do you want it to be?"

"What guy wouldn't want a booty call from a hot girl?"

I liked that this sexy, mysterious guy had called me hot, but it made me feel intimidated. I wasn't sure how to respond. A few minutes later, 'G' texted, "When are you coming over?"

I showed Nikki 'G's response and she jumped up and down. She said I had to go over and hook up with this guy for the mere fact that I had to find out why he was famous. I looked at my phone and Ben hadn't texted me back so I decided *fuck it* and I responded to 'G,' "What's your address?"

'G' sent me a text with his address. I hugged Nikki goodbye and headed out the door. I walked home and hopped in the shower to shave my legs and hairy muff real quick before hailing down a cab and heading to 'G's.

When I arrived at 'G's, I was a little nervous. I signed in at the front desk and the man behind the desk called up, confirming I was allowed up. I'd hoped the guy at the front desk would reveal 'G's full name or at least first name, but he didn't. He said, "'G,' Audrey is here to see you."

'G' gave the go-ahead for me to come up so I walked through the glass door and headed up to the 20th floor. When I arrived, I found condo 2004 and knocked on the door. 'G' opened the door and gave me a hug when I entered. He told me I looked beautiful while he helped me take my coat off, which made me smile. As I walked into 'G's condo, I looked for clues to find out this guy's real name. I even tried to peek at some mail on his kitchen counter, but I couldn't find any clues.

I sat down on the couch and 'G' offered me a glass of wine. I didn't need any more alcohol running through my blood, but I accepted. He poured us each a glass of wine and then sat next to me on the couch. Once seated, he asked, "What took you so long to call?"

I said, "Honestly, I forgot you'd given me your number until tonight when I was talking to my friend Nikki."

'G' said, "Ouch! You forgot about me? I didn't forget about you, but I couldn't call you because I didn't have your number."

I said, "Well, you knew about my book so I'm sure if you were really interested, you could've looked me up."

'G' said, "I did."

I asked, "You looked me up?"

"Well, I Googled you out of curiosity."

"What did you find?"

'G' smiled as he said, "I found that you write about sex, a lot."

"That is true. Is that bad?"

"Not at all, it's actually sexy."

I smiled and asked, "Oh, really?"

'G' said, "Yes, really," before kissing me.

I kissed 'G' back and his breath tasted better than any man I had kissed before. It probably tasted so amazing because even though I'd brushed my teeth when I went home to shave my legs and muff, my breath tasted terrible. His kiss was soft and the touch of his hands behind the back of my neck was gentle. While we were softly getting to know one another's lips, 'G' lightly lifted me off the couch and carried me into the bedroom.

In the bedroom, 'G' placed me on the bed before pulling off my pants. Once my pants were off, he crawled on top of me and began kissing me again. His scent and taste were such a turn-on. He didn't even need to touch me anywhere to get me wet. While on top of me, 'G' took his own shirt off and – damn, that boy was fine. His six-pack was more distinct than any I had ever seen. It made me believe this guy had to be an athlete of some kind.

With no shirt on, 'G' began kissing me again. While he was kissing me, he pulled my shirt off over my head. We had an awkward moment while he was pulling it off when it got stuck on my head, which caused a good laugh, but we quickly got back to kissing. 'G' moved away from my lips, down my neck, and past my breasts before he kissed my pussy. I took in the pleasure, not wanting him to stop, but he did. Because he didn't last down there long I worried that maybe I had a funky-smelling pussy, but remembered I had just showered so it couldn't be that bad.

When 'G' came up from licking my pussy, he said, "I just want to fuck you so hard."

As much as I enjoyed a nice calm munching of my rug, I was cool with just getting fucked. I wasn't here for some grand intimate moment. I had made a booty call so I wasn't expecting tender loving care of my pussy. 'G' went to push his hard cock into my pussy, but I stopped him and told him he needed to put a condom on. I didn't even know this guy's first name so if there was any time to be safe, now was the time.

'G' annoyingly put a condom on and then pushed his cock inside me. I moaned with pleasure, feeling the initial penetration. Once inside me, 'G' fucked me hard and deep. His cock was pretty large, but the pain from the size of his cock created pleasure within me. I watched his strong arms and abs flex while he fucked me, which was a big turn-on. They all flexed in such a sexy way. He fucked me for a few minutes then demanded I flip over and get on all fours. The way he yelled at me made me feel his control, which was a turn-on.

I got on all fours and 'G' pushed his cock back inside my pussy. He grabbed my hips with his hands, using them to move my body while he thrust his cock in and out of me. He yelled out, "You like when I fuck you, whore?" I didn't respond. I loved some dirty talk, but at the moment I was being a really big whore coming over here to fuck this stranger, and I took offense to what he said. Since I didn't respond, he seemed to get irritated and said, "I'm talking to you, slut! Do you like when I fuck you, whore?"

I was still feeling offended, but I quietly said, "Yes."

'G' said, "What did you say, you fucking whore?"

I said, "Yes, I like when you fuck me."

"Say it louder, whore." I didn't say anything back. For some reason I was regretting coming here and I legitimately started feeling like a whore. I wasn't liking the way I was feeling. 'G' said, "Oh, you don't want to respond? Fine, I'll make you scream, bitch."

'G' pulled his cock out of my pussy and then pushed it into my asshole with force and with no warning. I squealed like a pig. I had never felt so much pain in my life. After squealing, I pulled away from 'G' and got off the bed. I was fucking out of there. I felt like a disgusting whore and I didn't want to be there any longer. 'G' asked, "What the fuck are you doing, bitch?"

I said, "I'm out of here."

'G' said, "What - you can't handle a real man?"

I said, "You aren't a real man, you are a fucking asshole."

I put my clothes on as fast as I could and grabbed my coat on the way out of his condo's front door. When I got into the elevator, I started crying. I felt so dirty and disgusting. Once at the ground level, I wiped my eyes and walked outside to hail a cab, smiling at strangers as they passed by. I tried acting like I didn't feel like I had just been butt raped. When I got in the cab I told the cabbie my address and fought to hold the tears back while I tried to comfortably sit, because my asshole hurt so bad. I was so uncomfortable that it made the ten-minute cab ride feel like an hour.

When I got home I went into my bathroom and pulled down my pants. There was a little bit of blood on my underwear. I put on some comfy cotton granny panties and got a bag of peas out of the freezer. I set the peas down on a chair in the kitchen and sat down on them. The cold felt so good on my torn-open asshole. I put my head down on the table and cried.

The next morning I woke up and my asshole felt like it was on fire. On top of that I had some serious cramps. I went into the bathroom and as I undressed I noticed there was blood on my granny panties, but luckily it looked like period-blood and not asshole-blood. I turned around and bent over a little, trying to look at my asshole in the mirror. When I got a good view, I saw a bubble of sorts. It kind of looked like that little bubble you sometimes got in the knot of a balloon. *Fuck, I had a hemorrhoid!* Not only did I have my period and not only did my asshole hurt, but I had a fucking hemorrhoid, too. To make matters worse, when I took my shirt off to shower I saw the notorious nipple hair was back.

I stared at myself in the mirror for a moment, realizing the low I was in. What had I been doing these past couple of months? Having sex with a woman, blowing a guy for taking me on vacation, having sex with a guy whom I only knew as 'G', fucking another guy in an underground club, and avoiding the nice guy who just wanted to love me. Fuck, Ben was the kind of guy who wouldn't care about a notorious nipple hair; a guy who would buy me tampons at the store if I asked him to, and a guy who would put hemorrhoid cream on my asshole just to make me feel better.

I shook my head at myself in the mirror before I got into the shower. After I got out of the shower, I bundled up to walk down to the pharmacy to buy hemorrhoid cream, tampons, and wine. The young guy at the counter must've had a million things running through his head while he was ringing up my items. On my cold walk back, I thought about Ben. Here was this great guy who, for some fucking reason, just wanted to love and take care of me. What the hell was wrong with me? He was hot, we had good sex, and I had never laughed as hard with a guy like I laughed when I was with Ben.

As I walked up the stairs to my apartment, I decided I was ready to stop doing ridiculous things to keep myself from opening up to Ben. What was I scared of? Scared of moving to New York? Scared of taking a risk? Scared of commitment? Scared of getting hurt? It had to be the hurt thing. I had to remind myself that Ben was not Chase. Ben was a different breed. He didn't want to pull me into his world like Chase did; Ben wanted to create a world with me.

I pulled out my phone and looked at the last text message Ben text me. He said, "Sorry for getting back to you so late, darling, but I had to take a last-minute flight to London. I'll be back on the 18th. Hope you had a good night."

I'd never responded to Ben because I was too preoccupied getting my asshole destroyed by some guy named 'G.' I'd been acting so ignorantly. I tried to think of what to text Ben. I wanted it to be something brilliant to tell him that I was ready to dive in with him. I thought and thought for several minutes when I realized that this situation deserved more than a text. I should call him, but what would I say when I called him? I tried to put myself into Ben's shoes. What would he say if the roles were reversed? As I was thinking, I realized that I needed to build a story, like I did in my books, because Ben would build a story for me, much like he had on my first visit to New York City. I decided I needed backup for this plan because I wanted to build an amazing story. I texted Nikki and Bree in a group message saying, "911 come over now!"

Nikki arrived at my place ten minutes later

and Bree wasn't far behind. We all knew the 911 code and respected it. Even though it was only 11 a.m. on a Sunday morning, we started drinking the wine I'd bought at the pharmacy. Luckily, both Nikki and Bree had brought reinforcements. We sat down on the couch and I walked them through my asshole rape of an experience by the dishonorable 'G.' I then went on to explain the hemorrhoid, period, and nipple hair. They were surprisingly empathetic, but they also had a few chuckles. Once I'd explained the entire background of what had gone down, I told them I was ready to give it a go with Ben, but I wanted to do it in a grand way.

Nikki said it was easy and that all I needed to do was show up at his place naked with a sandwich in one hand and beer in the other. I agreed that would work, but I wanted to do something completely ridiculous because I knew if the roles were reversed, that's what Ben would do. We bounced ideas around and while we were brainstorming Bree screamed out, "Oh my God, his name is Ben Wright! He's your 'Mr. Wright,' Audrey!"

Nikki responded saying, "Wait, I have one too. He's 'Ben Wright' for you all along!"

Their wordplay made me laugh and smile, knowing that I had finally realized that "Mr. Wright" had walked into my life. I couldn't wait to tell Ben how I felt about him and have my turn to spoil him. I looked up dates of when athletic events were happening in New York when Bree came up with the idea to tie one of my favorite movies, *An Affair to Remember,* in with the situation. I loved the idea because it was New York, so it fit perfectly.

After several glasses of wine, we decided the plan would start with me sending a watch to Ben from Breitling, Ben's favorite watchmaker. With the watch I'd include a note that said, "It's our time. Meet me at the top of the Empire State Building at 5 p.m. on January 20th."

Drunk, I called and made the watch order to the New York store and they agreed to hand-deliver it with the note. After getting that part of the plan in play, I asked Nikki and Bree what else I could do and we decided the Knicks game was perfect since they were playing at Madison Square Garden that night. I hopped online and bought two courtside tickets. After that I needed to book a hotel so we Googled a few places and decided on the Crosby Street Hotel. I called the hotel and reserved a suite. I had the romantic moment at the Empire State Building, the game at Madison Square Garden and a super posh hotel all lined up. It seemed like an undeniable night of fun and romance to officially start a relationship together.

Everything was coming together. My period would be gone by the 20th, my hemorrhoid should be gone, and I had already tweezed out the notorious nipple hair. I wanted everything to be perfect for this because Ben was a man who deserved the best after all he had done for me. I decided that between now and then I'd have as little contact with Ben as possible because I am the world's worst secret keeper. He'd get the watch on the 18th, the day he returned from London. That was enough time for him to understand the situation. I hoped he wouldn't call and ask me questions about it, but instead he'd let it be and show up as instructed in the note.

The morning of January 20th I got up early and headed out of the door to O'Hare Airport. As I was walking out of my building I realized I hadn't packed any lingerie. What the fuck was wrong with me? This night called for my best lingerie. I walked back up to my apartment and grabbed my favorite lacy bra, stockings and panties. In my sexy drawer I noticed some lingerie that Chase had bought me. I took it out of the drawer and threw it out in the garbage on my way out. I was finally out of the door and on my way to New York City to seduce a man in a way in which I had never seduced a man before. The manager at Breitling had called me to confirm the watch had been delivered on the 18th so the game plan was playing out on cue so far. Since I had begun to devise the plan, the only contact Ben and I had had was through a couple of text messages. I thought it was good to have the space anyway, but I also knew that if we talked we'd end up talking about 'us' and I felt like it would be so much better to do it face-to-face.

I checked into the Crosby Street Hotel and asked them to have champagne sent up later that night. They were very accommodating. I was extremely nervous and I didn't know why. I knew Ben would be there with a smile and probably some ridiculous plan of his own. Before leaving the hotel I bundled up. It was snowing and freezing cold outside and I wanted to be prepared for much romance on the top of the Empire State Building.

I arrived at the Empire State Building a few minutes before 5 p.m. I sucked on a couple mints in preparation for passionate kisses. I took the elevator up and strolled around impatiently to kill the minutes before 5 p.m.. Once my phone said it was 5 p.m., I walked near the elevators, anxiously awaiting Ben's arrival, but several minutes passed and there was no sign of Ben. I thought maybe traffic or the fresh-falling snow was keeping him from being on time so I remained as patient as I could. More minutes passed and still no sign of Ben. I checked my phone for the twentieth time, but there was no word from Ben. I decided to take a wander around to distract myself.

Once 6 p.m. hit I began to worry that Ben wasn't coming. That maybe he wasn't serious about us and that it was all part of his game or maybe, just maybe, he'd been hit by a car on the way and was unable to walk. If that was the case though, he would've texted or called me. We lived in such a different time than when the movie *An Affair to Remember* took place. I stuck around longer because I didn't have to be anywhere else and my heart told me he'd be there.

When 7 p.m. rolled around Chuck, the security guard, asked me, "Are you still waiting, sweetheart?"

When I'd arrived I had told Chuck my plan and he had told me that many lovers had come to the Empire State Building before. I said to Chuck, "Yes, I am still waiting."

Chuck's response was, "I'm here to talk if you need me."

Finally, around 7:30 p.m. I decided to throw in the towel. I felt like an idiot the whole elevator ride down, but I began making excuses in my head for Ben's decision not to come. Ben had no idea that I had randomly gone to some famous guy's house to fuck a week ago when I was drunk, even though I didn't know the guy's name. If Ben had found out about that, well, that was enough to put someone off. On top of that, I hadn't contacted him much the past week.

The thing was, everything had been completely planned out and put in Ben's hands, but Ben hadn't shown up. So, unless he had been hit by a car on his way to the Empire State Building, there was no reason for him not to show up - unless he wasn't looking for what he said he was looking for. I wanted and needed excuses to make myself feel better, but I couldn't think of any good enough to explain his absence. I badly wanted to text him to confirm he'd got the watch and note or to simply find out why he wasn't on his way to see me. I even thought about having the cabbie take me to his condo to find out in person, but I didn't ask the cabbie to take me there. I asked the cabbie to take me back to the Crosby Street Hotel.

When I arrived at the hotel, I stopped in the bar for a glass of wine. I needed something to relax me and help me feel better about the romantic rejection that I had just experienced. I took down a glass in less than five minutes and requested a refill. Once refilled, I took my glass up to my room and cried. I had made my bed with all my stupid sexual endeavors and now I needed to lie in it. With my glass of wine, I went into the bathroom to fill up the huge bathtub. While it was filling up, I looked at myself crying in the mirror. I looked like complete shit. I don't know why, but for some reason watching myself cry like a fucking fool in the mirror made me feel better.

While I was watching myself cry in the mirror, there was a knock on the door to my hotel room. I got excited thinking that it could be Ben; that maybe something had happened to keep him from meeting me and he was here now because Nikki had let him in on the details of my whereabouts. Or, even better, he had run to the Empire State Building in a panic and Chuck the security guard had told him that I had been there, but had left to go back to my hotel so Ben had called every hotel in search of my reservation. Yeah, that sounded more dramatic and movie-like.

I threw on a white comfy robe and ran to the door, but when I opened the door it was room service with the champagne that I had ordered when I checked in. I welcomed the man in and he placed the champagne on the table before he exited. Once he was gone, I fell to the ground in tears. *Fucking shit. If only I had realized what a great guy I had in front of me a couple of weeks ago then I wouldn't be in this predicament and hurting so badly!*

I cried on the floor and continued to cry while I filled myself a glass of champagne. From there I took the tears back to the bathroom where I cried in the bathtub even longer. The entire time I wanted to call Ben, but knew that would be a bad idea because he'd decided not to show up. I wanted to know why he hadn't shown up so badly, but I kept reminding myself the point of the matter was that he hadn't shown up.

I crawled into bed and tried to cry myself to sleep, but I knew sleep wasn't going to be happening anytime soon. I had too much emotion stirring in my body. I decided to pull out my laptop and write. I started from the beginning when I'd shit my pants because I was such a hot mess from getting my heart trampled all over by Chase. I went on and on from there. I explained the random Facebook message from Ben and everything that had gone down with my memoir, *Dating Chase Walker*, getting published. For three days I sat in my hotel room writing away and ordering room service like a chore.

I never called Ben. He texted me, asking if I was okay, and called me once, but I didn't answer and he didn't leave a voicemail. I considered calling him back a thousand times, but I never did. He hadn't shown up and then he wanted to know if I was okay? I was feeling a sense of anger toward him inside and I needed to get over that before I could talk to him. Nikki and Bree were texting me like crazy, asking how it went, but I never responded. In fact, I communicated only with room service for three days. Never leaving my room and never even showering, I wrote and wrote until I got to this point; the point at which my romantic comedy-esque story ends. The point at which I got rid of my infatuation with Chase and let go of the possibility of love with Ben. The point at which it is time for me to check out of this hotel and get back to reality in Chicago. The point from which my life must go on and the idea of a crazy romance of a love just ended up making for a good story.

So here I sit, writing the ending of what could have been. Or maybe better said, what could have 'Ben.' Writing the words of a story that I so badly wish was my reality again and kicking myself for not letting Ben in sooner. Even though I am angry and hurt Ben didn't show up, I can't blame him. He just wanted to love me and I toyed with him for months while I whored it up with strangers from the East Coast to the West Coast. New York, I want to love you, but I will close this computer, finally take a shower, check out of this hotel, and get back to reality in Chicago.

"We all want to be loved, don't we? Everyone looks for a way of finding love. It's a constant search for affection in every walk of life."
    -Audrey Hepburn